THE
BUSINESS
PROPOSAL

THE
BUSINESS
PROPOSAL

NATHANIEL K. GEE

SWEETWATER BOOKS
An imprint of Cedar Fort, Inc.
Springville, Utah

ISBN 13: 978-1-4621-3905-7

Published by Sweetwater Books, an imprint of Cedar Fort, Inc.
2373 W. 700 S., Springville, UT 84663
Distributed by Cedar Fort, Inc., www.cedarfort.com

Library of Congress Control Number: 2021933514

Cover design by Shawnda T. Craig
Cover design © 2021 Cedar Fort, Inc.
Edited by Hali Bird and Valene Wood

Printed in the United States of America

10 9 8 7 6 5 4 3 2 1

Printed on acid-free paper

In 2004, after a two-year hiatus from dating, an awkward young man walked into his sister's college apartment and met her roommates. His world was that of logic and practicality. He had no room for the arts, and he didn't see much use for their study or profession. But one roommate's artistic nature and love of a world he was blind to captured his attention.

Jeanine, thank you for helping me realize that a world with only raw facts and figures is missing the most important elements it has to offer. You have become my world and I owe this work and all my greatest accomplishments to you. Because of you, I am ecstatic for what tomorrow, next year, and eternity will bring.

Chapter 1

The Professionals

Eye contact is a powerful thing. Empathy, love, passion, confusion, distress, panic, and a plethora of other emotions can all be conveyed between the nose and eyebrows. Pure disdain was the message Mr. Johnson's eyes were sending since the moment he walked into the office of Dr. Byron Lewis. But, to ensure the message wasn't lost in translation, Mr. Johnson sent it over and over again.

The forced presence of husbands in their office was something all marriage counselors were accustomed to. But in Byron's experience, Mr. Johnson usually dealt with this by simple indifference. No, something was clearly on the man's mind beyond his disintegrating marriage. This was something more.

As Mrs. Johnson told a story about how Mr. Johnson ignored her during their last therapy assignment, which was to discuss why she was originally attracted to him, Mr. Johnson did a superb job of reenacting his indifference to her. He focused completely on the doctor. Byron was usually a very conscientious listener, but it was hard to focus on Mrs. Johnson's words with Mr. Johnson's glare demanding so much attention.

Byron pressed on, "So, Mr. Johnson, why do you think Mrs. Johnson feels you weren't listening?"

Mr. Johnson paused, then said, "I'm not sure. Does your wife ever assume you're not listening?"

Clients often tried to get Byron to interject his personal life, some were innocent, but increasingly, these requests were less about curiosity and were more of a sinister nature. But, treating it as innocent, he said, "It's important we focus on your situation."

"Oh, okay. Well, since you don't want to talk about your situation," Mr. Johnson's tone had not improved, "I guess this is my session so we will only talk about mine. So, why didn't she think I was listening? I may have not had good eye contact. Isn't eye contact important?"

His eyes continued to pierce into Byron, proving that at least under certain situations, Mr. Johnson's aptitude for eye contact left nothing to be desired. "Yes, that is important, but could it have been more than that?" Byron was doing everything in his power to avoid what he knew would turn into an awkward situation. Yet deep down Byron knew what was coming, it was happing more and more recently.

"Or maybe I was stressed. You ever have a stressful day?"

Byron at that particular moment was very prepared to answer this question, but before he could tell himself to hold his tongue, Mr. Johnson added. "What do you do when you get home all stressed and your wife wants to talk?"

"Again, Mr. Johnson, let's focus on your situation."

"Okay, but I want to know what you do when you are in *my* situation."

Directly trying to maneuver away from his personal life was clearly not going to work so he tried the old, answer-the-question-they-should-have-asked response, "Your wife deserves open, honest conversation. So, if you need a break after work to de-stress, be open about it."

Mrs. Johnson at this point began to interject, "But this was on a Satur—"

"How would you know?" Mr. Johnson cut her off, demanding all the attention the little office could offer.

"What?" Byron expected some confrontation, but this was more than he imagined.

Recomposing himself a little, Mr. Johnson clarified, "How would you know? Have you tried it?"

Byron straightened up and made himself as big as he could get. "I have a doctorate from the University of Connecticut, worked for one of the most prestigious clinics in America and counseled hundreds of couples. I am very qualified to discuss these situations."

Mr. Johnson's face relaxed. He smiled and sat back into his chair and said, "And yet with all that, no real experience. Come on, Jen, let's get out of here." He stood and did the only thing he ever wanted to do from the first day he had walked into this office: walked out for the last time. Mrs. Johnson looked at her husband and then back to Byron, then back to her husband and once more to Byron. But the heap of mangled ego that was left of Byron was far from the pillar she would have needed to help sway her decision. The only strength was leaving the room and she followed it.

It was not the fact that a disgruntled client walked out that left Byron so worn. He had faced it before and would face it again. It was the increased frequency of such occurrences. It was no mystery to Byron where Mr. Johnson had discovered the fact that in matters of love, Byron was a bit of a novice. He had always avoided bringing his personal life into his work. He told clients that they didn't see family photos in his office because he didn't want to focus on his situation but theirs. But that all changed when a client, who blamed Byron for his failed marriage, had used his knowledge of Byron's bachelorhood to flood the internet with scathing reviews like, "Why does a man who has never said, *I do,* get to tell me what *to do* in my marriage." If Byron hadn't been so devastated, he would have had to admit, that one was pretty clever. Since these had picked up, his clients had dropped off. There were always men who were looking for a way to get out of counseling, but Byron prided himself on the fact that if they just gave him a chance, he could help. He had saved so many marriages that started their counseling with reluctance. Would they stop giving him that chance now that they had their out?

Inaction was not something Byron ever accepted. Every problem had a solution, as the Johnsons' footsteps faded away suddenly it was crystal clear. The solution was easy. "Yes, it wasn't mainstream, but that didn't make it wrong," his mind quickly countered. He always counseled his clients not to make life changing decisions under the duress of hurt feelings. His counsel echoed in his mind as he found himself rationalizing an irrational life choice. He felt himself dig in his heels for the same reason many others had ignored his counsel:

because he wanted to. The only question was the method to deliver the message. The internet made the options and reach almost unlimited. Foreign market was fairly good. No, better keep it close to home. It took only a few minutes to create a new Hotmail account and, surprisingly, no one had taken the handle yourhusband@hotmail.com. Next, he went to the Gazette Classifieds and put out an ad, "Local professional seeks wife."

Chapter 2

The Ad

J ulie rushed into her favorite café.

"Sorry I'm . . . "

"Late again?" Her best friend Becky interjected as she sat at the table across from her. "I planned on it. You're having tuna on rye with the minestrone soup."

"Minestrone soup? It can't be Wednesday already!"

"No Jules, it's Tuesday," Becky replied dryly. This was clearly another subtle attack on her 'too rigid routine,' one of their many over-discussed topics. After years of trying to get her friend to loosen up with persuasion, it seemed Becky now resorted to flat out defiance. At least, Julie felt it was unlikely she could forget which meal she took on Tuesdays after three years of eating lunch together.

"Well, I suppose I'll have to take Tuesday's lunch tomorrow. Maybe this way the waiter will actually get me my food before I have to request a to-go box."

Just then a waiter showed up with their food.

"You know," Becky began, "if your boss keeps you at the office till 12:10, he shouldn't expect you back until 1:10. Maybe you should talk to him about that. I really miss the days when we could relax and enjoy our lunch break. On to more important things though, tonight is your big date!"

"No, I'm pretty sure my last date was my biggest date: 300 pounds big. Photoshop is definitely the cupid of internet romance," Julie replied.

"And you probably didn't list 'bitterly pessimistic' under your profile either, so he wasn't the only one stretching the truth," Becky said.

"I think you mean, shrinking the truth," Julie said.

"Come on!" Becky censured, "That date was over a year ago. And you're going to love Ricky."

"I am not going tonight, Becky. I don't feel up to another blind date. You know I never said I would go."

"But you never stopped me from talking about it, and I would call that a passive agreement. You are my smartest and best-looking friend and, as much as I hate to admit it, you are the only one I know worthy of Ricky. Plus, Mark and I have been working on setting you up for months now, and tonight's all set. Ricky is showing up at your door at six whether you like it or not, so you really ought to be ready. Plus, if it doesn't work out with Ricky, I found you another guy."

"I haven't even gone on this date and you already have another guy?"

Becky slid a portion of the newspaper across the table.

Julie blinked several times and read it again. Who could possibly be willing to pay $500 a month for a wife he has no contact with? The ad was so strange that she took a second look to make sure this was the real paper and not a hoax Becky had put together. After her short inspection, she determined it was indeed authentic. "He's probably an immigrant who needs citizenship to keep his job."

"And why would an immigrant leave no room for divorce?" Becky asked. "I think he's an OBGYN who doesn't want to come across as a pervert."

"No way, you don't have to be married to be a respectable OB," Julie retorted.

"Well, whatever the case, if Ricky doesn't work out, then this could be your answer," Becky smirked. "No more invasive mother, no more dates with weirdos, and hey—supplement your income!"

"Yeah, just marriage to a weirdo—and not even real marriage. Thank you, but no. I'm not this desperate."

"Well, I'm disappointed, Jules. I was going to start a new job as a wife hunting agent with you as my first client. If it had worked out, I could charge a 15% fee. That comes to . . . " Becky paused, "$55 a month." Math was never her strong point. "Just think, you could pay my internet bill every month."

"Your internet bill for my self-respect. I don't think so," Julie replied.

"Oh, well, since you aren't interested in an extra $500 a month, I had better go back to my day job. I will let you know if any higher offers come in. And in all seriousness, be ready on time: Ricky likes punctuality." She finished her last comment in a hurried fashion, grabbed her bag, and placed some money on the table.

Julie knew her friend's rush was to avoid letting her make any derogatory statements, but Julie was determined, and as Becky got up, she said, "Why should I care what Ricky likes?"

Becky pretended not to hear as she walked out of the cafe.

Julie began to pick up her things while she casually placed her money on the table. As she did, a large man, noticeably Julie's senior, approached her from a nearby table. He was short and mostly bald, and his teeth told her he had smoked for most of his life.

"Excuse me, miss."

Julie hoped he was telling her she had dropped something, but she could guess why he was approaching. Why were the only men who approached her old and creepy?

"Yes?" she replied sounding as indifferent as possible.

"Miss, as I was eating my lunch, I happened to notice you and was quite taken with your elegance."

Elegance, huh? She hadn't heard that one before. When she thought of elegance, she thought of women from the 1800's with big dresses and. . . . but, a compliment is a compliment.

"Thanks," she said as she began to walk out. She knew men didn't approach women to simply tell them that they're elegant. Compliments from men were sure signs of them wanting something, and Julie was not in the giving spirit. But before her goal of ending the conversation with a quick exit was realized, he continued.

"Let me introduce myself," he said, hindering her progress. "My name is Harold." He put his hand out.

Her mind raced trying to figure how to get out of this interchange. She went ahead and shook his hand while the wheels turned.

He gave an expectant look as they shook, obviously expecting her name in return. The moment grew more awkward as silence continued: he, waiting for a name, and she, too busy trying to think of how to get out of there to realize it was her turn to talk.

Finally, Harold continued, and she was relieved as he let go of the hand, "Well, I will be in town over the next week. We should meet sometime, maybe here . . . tomorrow . . . for lunch?"

This was usually where Julie would simply say, "I'm sorry, I'm dating someone." She used it so frequently that it no longer bothered her that there was no truth to it, but she worried that he may have overheard some of her earlier conversation, which took the boyfriend excuse off the table. But thinking of tables made Julie notice that the tables in this establishment were very top heavy. While she had eaten here many times, she had never noticed just how unbalanced they appeared, rather like a hippo on a unicycle. With this thought came the almost involuntary sway of her hip bumping the table. The table, a chair, and all it contained, quickly found the floor. The crash caused all heads in the diner to turn her way.

"Allow me!" Harold's chivalry kicked in like clockwork and as he bent down, she got out. As she dashed down the street, her first thought was one of sheer victory. However, as her distance from the café became comfortable and the relief of being away from Harold diminished, a sick feeling took the victory's place. She felt bad for Harold, the café's broken dishes, and the fact that she wouldn't be able to eat at her favorite café with Becky for a couple weeks because

Harold might be there. Her mother always said that if she spent half the time trying to find men as she did avoiding them, she would have been married long ago. What her mother didn't seem to realize was just how many men out there were worth avoiding, and Julie was beginning to wonder if there were any worth finding. It was her experience the more men she found, the more men she had to find ways to avoid.

The debate between the side of her that wanted companionship and the side that disliked almost every man she dealt with continued to battle within her flustered brain, with interruptions now and then by the echoes of her mother's advice, "give them a chance, having a man around can change everything." She was relieved when she finally made it back to the office. As she sat down at her desk, her practical side told the other two sides to stop their endless bickering so she could get some work done.

"Hey, Juju bug," Larry said, inviting himself into her office.

Larry was someone who qualified as a man she worked to avoid. The fact that he worked in her office though, made it rather difficult. "The name is Julie, or rather Ms. Smith, if you don't mind."

"Well anyways, JuJu, I have got two tickets to see Garth Brooks this weekend, and I know you love country," he said as he waved the tickets in the air like they were hundred-dollar bills.

"I'm seeing someone Larry, you know that," she lied.

"Oh, he won't mind friends getting together to enjoy the concert. Of course, if it makes you feel uncomfortable, feel free to break up with him first," Larry said as he sat on her desk is his skinny jeans that made his 120 pounds look even smaller.

She gave him an irritated glare that would have clearly conveyed the meaning of "Get out!" to anyone with any sense. But in doing so, she forgot who she was dealing with.

"So, what do you say?" he quipped.

"No, my boyfriend would kill you. So, while there is an upside, I still don't want to."

"Come on, Julie, these are great seats. Give me a chance." He only called her Julie when he got desperate or when the boss was around.

"Larry, you have to accept that I'm dating someone else. If that changes, I will let you know," she said as definitively as she could.

Larry showed a smile and simply said, "Everyone knows you really don't have a boyfriend."

His cool confidence worried Julie. Could it be true? Did everyone know? Yes, the lie was her tool to push off Larry's endless pursuits, but it was so convenient that she started to use it for more than just avoiding Larry. Coworkers trying to set her up . . . out came the boyfriend. Dinner party at the bosses place . . . boyfriend planned a nice night. Did they all know it was a sham?

"What do you mean? Of course, I have a boyfriend. You think I just made him up?"

"Oh, I don't know. What's his name?"

She paused, in all this time she had never been asked his name and never thought to make one up either. It may be one of the miracles of the human brain that hers literally had thousands of male names in its database, yet at this crucial moment it was able to keep access to such data just beyond the reach of her tongue. She finally shot back, "It's none of your business what his name is."

Clearly the pause had done its damage. "Forget his name, huh? Quite a boyfriend," Larry said, half laughing. "I have also noticed that you've been dating he-who-must-be-left-nameless for years and yet no pictures.

Even with things going south, she wasn't about to give up her favorite excuse. "Even though he dislikes cameras, my boyfriend would not want me seeing Garth with someone else." She stated this with as much of a 'case closed' attitude as she could.

"Well, let me know if you change your mind," he said as he practically skipped out of the office.

Julie was left alone with the sad realization that what Larry vocalized was most likely going on in everyone's mind.

She needed to prove she had a boyfriend. Didn't she have a friend or relative who could pose as a boyfriend? A few pictures would go a long way. The sad part was she couldn't think of any guys she knew well enough to pose in the photos. Perhaps she could just meet a guy one night at a bar and pretend to be interested long enough to get a few good pictures. There was Joe who always delivered her takeout. Maybe while he counted her tip, she could snap a picture?

As her mind raced over ways to prove her imaginary boyfriend existed, she suddenly woke up to reality. Why was she so desperate to perpetuate this lie? Being single was no crime. She didn't need to come up with some elaborate hoax. She didn't even want a boyfriend.

But there was her mother. Even with as big of an annoyance as Larry was, he didn't compare to good old mom. Her mother was relentless. She came from the old school of thought that any girl who isn't married by age thirty was destined for a life of loneliness and misery—not to mention financial destitution. Julie hadn't been reminded of her age so much in one year since she was four. "You are thirty, you know. Men don't want to date a girl much over thirty because her birthing window is closing quickly. Men want to have an heir you know . . . " She wasn't sure where her mother got this, probably a History channel special on Henry VIII. Did she have to alter her life just to appease her mother, push off Larry, and avoid all the Harolds out there?

Tonight would be her first date in over a year. The last being a blind date she met online that made her sick, both metaphorically and physically. Not only did he look nothing like his online profile picture, but they had eaten at a restaurant that served Mexican-Chinese Fusion. It was shut down by the health department a week later. Later that night in her bathroom as the water chestnuts in Spanish rice made their way back to her mouth, she made a vow to never go on another blind date in her life.

That promise quickly put an end to her dating life and increased the need for the imaginary boyfriend excuses. Only Becky, who could probably convince her to bungee jump, eventually wore her down. And now she was about to be on a date with Ricky, a widower. His wife had passed a few years back in a tragic accident. The very word widower made her think of a grey-haired man with a cane. But he couldn't be that old given that Becky's husband had been friends with him in high school. And just to prove he was okay, Becky had brought pictures and stories to convince Julie. It was true, he sounded normal, looked very handsome, and didn't carry a cane. He was six feet tall with dark hair and brown eyes. Not fat, not bald, and not twice her age. He didn't even live with his parents.

While she didn't expect it, she was hopeful her blind date tonight would go well. She didn't expect to get that boyfriend she'd been telling everyone about, but she wouldn't mind a guy friend. Maybe one she could get a few pictures with.

Chapter 3

The Blind Date

The doorbell rang a few minutes before six o'clock. "Well, he's certainly prompt," Julie thought.

She opened the door to see Ricky, who looked older than she expected. His graying temples indicated years that Jill's pictures had not shown. It wasn't a bad thing; Julie actually preferred a man with some wisdom.

"So, you must be Julie," Ricky said with a smile.

"And you're Ricky."

He paused. "Well, I guess I am."

Julie raised her eyebrows. It was pretty rare that people forgot their own name. Seeing her concern, he quickly said, "I'll explain on the way. Shall we?" He offered Julie his arm.

She looked down and, with a small smile, took his arm. She felt very fifties doing it but made a note that the fifties must have been a fairly nice time to live. "Thank you," she said as they headed for the car. He opened both the gate and the car door. He did it so naturally that Julie guessed he must date often, he was just too good at it to not be well-practiced.

Once they were on their way, Ricky began to explain his pause at the door. "Ricky is my name, sort of, but I'm not used to being called that. Marky has been calling me that long before he had even met Becky.

"See, in high school, I thought Ricky sounded cooler than Rich or Richard, so I went with it. When I got to college, I realized that being cool wasn't so important, so I dropped it. But to Marky, I will always be Ricky."

"What would you like me to call you?" Julie asked.

"Oh, it's up to you, but most people call me Rich."

"Rich it is."

"So, what about you? Should I call you Julie or something else?"

Julie was already beginning to like Rich, and she would rather he call her "Jules," but worried it would sound too much like a pet name. So, even though she was thinking, "Tell him to call you Jules," she said quickly, "Julie is fine."

"So, what kind of music do you like?" he said, obviously using a preplanned chip at the ice.

Knowing that Larry was still anxious to take her to see Garth Brooks and fearing he may have her bugged, she went against country. "I like classical." That was a safe answer and made her look smart.

"Oh, I never could get into classical. I guess I've always thought only old people liked it." Ouch, strike one, thought Julie. At least he's honest, I mean, who really is gutsy enough to admit they hate classical?

"Do you like monster ballads?" Rich offered.

"You mean, like guys with long hair, tights, and lipstick singing love songs?" Julie asked.

"Uh, I guess I've never thought of them like that, but yeah."

He handed her a black binder-like object. "Are these CD's? I didn't know people still listened to these. Well, let's see what you got." Julie flipped through Rich's CD case.

Metallica, Led Zeppelin, ACDC . . . Clearly, if they had something in common, it was not going to be music. She was about to give up when she got near the end.

"Wait a minute, is this Celine Dion?" she said.

"Oh, is that in there?" he said, rather embarrassed. "I swear it was planted there by my enemies."

"Well, thank goodness for your enemies," she said as she popped the disc into the CD player.

He smiled.

"So, besides listening to bad music, what do you like to do?" he asked.

She remembered now why she didn't like first dates. What could she really say to that? She liked to watch TV, but she couldn't say that. Talking to friends, uh, that wasn't much better. I like to run marathons . . . that wasn't true. Knowing that a lie might come back to bite her, she went with, "I like to cook." This was sort of true—she did know how to cook.

"Really? What's your specialty?"

"Oh, I try different things, but mostly I cook saucy food."

"Saucy?"

"I mean like Asian food . . . with sauces." Her face was redder than any Asian sauce available on the market.

"I am actually quite skilled at eating Asian food with sauces." Rich gave her a sly smile.

Their conversation kept a steady pace all the way to the Cheesecake Factory, where they were meeting Mark and Becky. Julie and Rich walked in to find their friends already seated.

"Glad you both made it," Becky said as she saw them approach. "Sit down, we have some appetizers coming."

"Hey Ricky, did you drive the Mustang?" Mark asked, with wide eyes.

"You know I won't take that car out of the garage when I am anywhere near you," Rich replied.

"You could've picked me up in a Mustang?" Julie asked, turning away to feign being hurt.

Mark added, "Not just any Mustang, but a '67 Mustang. The same one we had in high school."

"*We* had? I think you meant to say, the Mustang that *I* had. I did make the mistake of letting you drive it once. That led to the only non-original part that car has, the driver's side door."

"Oh, look, the food is here," Mark said.

"I want to hear the story," Julie requested.

"It's not my husband's proudest moment," Becky said.

Rich flashed a huge smile as he began. "Marky pulled up after taking it for a drive and saw Jill Schlesinger. He got the bright idea of calling out to her to give her a ride. She didn't hear him, so he got out to wave her down and left the door open without the parking brake on. The car rolled back past a gate at the school, and the door got ripped off." Rich chuckled. "And I couldn't even be mad, because I was the crazy guy who let him borrow the car."

"Mark and I have a tendency of having things we love most damaged by close friends," Becky said raising her eyebrows.

"I said sorry, we don't need to bring it up now," Julie said as she felt her cheeks begin to warm.

"I think it's a perfect time to bring it up," Mark said. "I lost him his precious door, what did you do?"

"It is completely not my fault. It's only because Becky is such a good cook."

"Oh, sweetening me up won't stop me from telling the story." Becky leaned in as the story began. "You may not know this, but Mark and I got first and second place in a regional science fair in sixth grade. We didn't even know each other and it wasn't until we had been married for a few years that we put the pieces together. Sure enough, my mom had saved the local paper that had Mark and I standing together. It was the coolest thing. She gave it to me and I show people because it's the coolest, most priceless, wonderful . . . "

"Okay we get the idea," Julie interrupted.

"Well, we were having Julie over for dinner for the first time and I pulled out the paper to show her and she . . . " Becky tried to hold back the laughter. Julie closed her eyes in shame. "Drooled on it."

"What?" Rich asked.

"Right on our picture, a big drop of drool."

"I was so embarrassed, but like I said, the dinner was really good and maybe you shouldn't get it out while you are feeding people?" Julie said.

They all laughed. "Well, the good news is now that paper gives us two great stories, and it is safely behind a clear plastic protector." As Becky finished, she got up and said, "I need to use the restroom," as she stared at Julie.

Julie looked back as to say, "What?" Becky gritted her teeth. "Julie, care to join me?"

Julie said, "Oh," she got up and said, "I'll go too, just in case Becky forgets to wash her hands."

Once out of earshot, Becky started in. "So, what do you think?"

Julie wanted to be coy but decided she wouldn't be any good at it. "He is actually normal."

"Wow, normal. Such a glowing review."

"Okay, he is better than normal. I think I kind of like him."

"What, did I just hear Julie, cold-hearted, man-eating Julie, say she thinks she kind of likes someone?" Becky teased.

"Speaking of glowing reviews, thanks for the cold-hearted, man-eating label."

"Okay, you aren't that bad, but I don't usually hear you say you like a guy! I can't wait for the wedding!"

"You just keep quiet and don't ruin it for me," Julie said, joking. Becky's big mouth was one of her best qualities, but it could also be her worst and Julie worried it was more the latter when it came to her chances with Rich.

The rest of the dinner date flew by in a whirlwind of laughter and chatter. The date plans had been restricted to only dinner, at Julie's insistence. She was so used to blind dates going badly that she didn't want to prolong the pain. Now, as Rich drove her home, she regretted this decision.

Once they pulled up to Julie's house, Rich, as he had been all night, was the perfect gentleman and opened her door. They walked together toward the porch, and Julie thought she better speak first. "Rich, I had a great time."

"Yeah, it was a lot of fun," he said casually.

They paused at the doorstep.

"Well, it's been a long time since I said good night on my doorstep. I usually just meet my dates where we're going," she said with a smile.

"I guess it has been a long time for me too," Rich said.

There was a pause, and Julie hoped Rich would ask for a second date, but all he said was, "Thanks again, Julie," and he gave her a quick hug.

It was ending. The date would end, and she wanted to see Rich again. It looked like he was about to say good night, so Julie blurted out, "We should do this again soon." His facial expression made her immediately regret it. If nothing were said, she'd have hope but she felt that being snuffed out as he spoke.

"Julie, I had a good time, but . . . " He paused. *Oh, here we go,* Julie thought.

Rich continued, "Marky asked if I would be willing to try a blind date. I thought I was ready, but after tonight I'm convinced, I'm not. That Celine Dion CD in the back of my case was Rachel's. Tonight was fun, don't get me wrong, but it made me miss Rachel too much," he said. "I'm not sure when or if I'd want to do this again." His voice trailed off.

Julie jumped in. "I completely understand, that makes perfect sense."

There was an awkward pause, as neither knew what else to say. Rich broke the silence, "Well, good night, Julie, thanks again." He walked back to his car.

Julie watched as he drove away. Once his brake lights faded into the distance, she rushed inside, collapsed onto the couch, and began to cry. Part of her was angry at herself for crying. She had just met the guy! Earlier today, she had been happy, and nothing much had changed since then.

She hated that she had allowed her emotions to get wrapped up in a man she hardly knew. She hated that she had to keep lying to her mom, Larry, and Harold. Why couldn't she just be happily single? Why did she have to date? Her emotions were rushing through her, and she now found herself far more caught up with emotions than she expected but she allowed the feelings to flow as she half sobbed, "If I were married, my mom wouldn't pester me all day! If I were married, Larry would leave me alone! If I were married, Harold wouldn't approach me! If I were married, there would be no blind dates, and if I were married, I wouldn't have awkwardly messed everything up with Rich!"

With the last statement she broke out into sobs again. After a few moments, she began to calm down. She didn't think she believed half of what she said, but it felt good to get it out. She didn't really have any desire to be married. What she really wanted was to be single and have everyone else think she was married.

As she sat up, her gaze went to the newspaper lying where she usually left it, half read, out on the coffee table. Her mind shot back to her earlier conversation with Becky and the strange ad. She picked up the classified section, turned to the ad, and read it again. This time she had a very different perspective.

This time he didn't seem strange. He sounded wise. This was likely a man in the same situation she was in. Of course he was. Surely hundreds must be in their situation. He wasn't crazy, but courageous. He was brave enough to do something she wished she had the guts to do, even if it wasn't socially acceptable.

She grabbed the paper and headed for the computer. She had secretly speculated that, after the date with Rich, she might have a boyfriend. What better consolation than landing a fiancé?

Chapter 4

The Breakup

Byron headed to the computer. It was two days ago that he had run his ad. Over those two days, he flipped-flopped back and forth between thinking he was insane or brilliant. He considered not opening the email account and let the whole thing disappear. The email was set up under a false name, and he figured the FBI could have traced it to him, but no one else could. Ignoring the email would let the entire thing wash over, but he had already taken the next two days off work to filter through emails and interview candidates. Even more than that, he knew his curiosity demanded that he check the email. He promised himself he wouldn't check them the first day, but he would have broken that promise yesterday at work if he hadn't left the password to this new email at home.

Now that the moment was upon him, he wondered if anyone even wrote him. If they didn't, he would have two days off. He was thinking that he might go visit San Diego when the mailbox opened and he saw that he had 221 messages. Perhaps he should have taken a whole week off.

The first email was from Star Jewell. Apparently, he wasn't the only one making up names. As soon as he opened the email, a large photo of "Star" in a Star Trek outfit appeared on his screen. Star Trek was not his thing, but he knew it well enough to recognize that she was trying to be Commander Troi from Star Trek generations. There was text below that he didn't need to read as it became the first to the trash bin.

The next email was from Natalia Swetlana. "I love be your wife. In America, I be honor you for death." Byron wasn't sure if this was Natalia's poor English or google translator's poor programming, but either way he wondered how Natalia had found his town's classifieds and how many other foreign brides, anxious for a ticket to America, were in the next 219 emails. A foreign bride did offer some advantages, but at some point, even with the poor immigration system, she would eventually make it to America, and then where would she go? No, he would stick to the domestic market.

Bambi Jones was next in line. With a sigh he began reading, "We don't need to get married to have a good time." Delete.

In rapid succession, the next thirty emails fell into the category of either foreign bride or too bohemian for him, and therefore all fell into the trash bin. Onto email number thirty-three, "I would be interested in your proposal. Let's meet." Flipping through the emails as quickly as he had, he had stopped reading names. So, after verifying that that was indeed all she had sent, no photo, nothing about her, no attachment, simply that she would be interested, he went back and got her name. Jennifer was this very short-winded writer. Had her email been first it would already be in the trash bin, but the last thirty emails had changed him. What he would have called lazy and lacking any pertinent data half an hour ago was classified as not inappropriate, not strange, and not solely interested in his citizenship. The more he thought about it, the more he realized if he had responded to his ad, he would have been similarly brief. So, it became the first email to avoid a quick demise and he went back to the rest.

The rest went very much the same as the first batch and by the time he had reviewed all the emails, only three remained, and all three shared Jennifer's attribute of brevity. The only thing that had been added was one email started by adding the kind words, "This is nuts but . . . " The other thing the other two emails shared was a first name, Julie. They became, nuts Julie and regular Julie.

It was a bit depressing that the only ones he could see having any chance of being his bride were the ones he knew absolutely nothing about. What was the likelihood that if he actually knew something about these three that they would still be in the running? But they had made it this far, so the three J's were to move on to round two. Now, for the first time, Byron was forced to ask himself, "What was round two?"

Should he try to get more information with a back and forth on email? Given how skeptical these three were, he could see it turning into a game of "you tell me first." The next option was to have them come to his office and simply go for a formal interview, but something told him formal was not the way to go, plus he thought he better avoid his office. Trying to explain this to Ms. Whittaker, his admin assistant, would be as comfortable as answering his hygienist question, "So, have you been flossing?" Also, depending on how the interview went, he wasn't sure he would want these women knowing exactly who he was, what he did, and where he worked. "Trust is the foundation on which a good marriage is built." He had said it thousands of times, and as he could hear himself saying it, he knew his new relationship was on a path to make the leaning tower of Pisa's substructure appear robust.

No, an interview style would not be best. Rather a nice sit-down meal together, three girls, three meals, breakfast, lunch, and dinner, or rather, late breakfast, lunch, and early dinner. He didn't want to be sitting around downtown with nothing to do. But how to be recognized. Forty thousand years ago a male Neanderthal was to meet a female Neanderthal at a cave party and wanted to know how he would pick her out. The decision was made that they would each wear a flower, and as safety pins had not been invented, they needed a flower that would attach to their leopard skin mumu's easily. It was a toss-up between thistle and rose. And in a decision that would define how single people determine who is anxious enough to find a mate as to label themselves with plants, they went with rose. Historians will debate how society would be different today if they would have chosen thistle but rose it was. And for Byron, a single red rose it would be. So, this Friday, three times, three restaurants, and one rose. He figured they wouldn't mind if he reused it.

The marble hallways were wide. The paintings were not replicas—beautiful, unique, and complementary to the surroundings. The hallways of the conference area inside the Bellagio were one of his favorite locations and on Fridays or weekends they rarely had any conferences going on, this left the vast hallways all to himself.

While his pessimistic, or maybe realistic, side didn't give him any better chance of this working out than the millions of gamblers whose money had paid for the lavish furnishings that surrounded him, his romantic side was willing to give it a chance, and that is what had led him to choosing a location he loved so much. The next corner would end his solitude. That is where the conference portion of the hotel ended and the day-to-day traffic of gamblers, diners, and hotel patrons began. Shortly after joining the fray, he beheld his destination, Bellagio Patisserie, a little French place behind the hotel's conservatory, tucked next to the largest chocolate fountain in the world. Anyone who has had a dessert from Bellagio Patisserie will not soon forget it. Each one was an artistic masterpiece. These are the kind of desserts people took pictures of before Facebook and Instagram so degraded the art of food photography.

Finding a seat, he looked at his phone, 10:50, ten minutes early was, in his view, perfectly on time. Verifying his rose was in place, he began to look for its match. Though many have waited much longer, ten minutes felt like a long time to wait for the woman who might be his wife to walk into the picture. Odd looks began to float his way as he tried to focus on each new woman that entered his view, searching each of their persons over to see if somewhere she bore a rose.

It was now 11:02, ten minutes had seemed eternally long, but he had at least known when that would end, now that the clock had rolled past 11:00, the clock actually slowed even further. How long he would wait until he simply gave up crossed his mind when he saw it, a single red rose. She was breathtaking. However, it is important to note that in the English language we don't always think of words based on their definition. Case in point, breathtaking. Someone can be so amazingly beautiful that seeing them for the first time causes the viewer to unexpectedly forget how to breathe. But being hit by a 350 pounds lineman may also be breathtaking. In this case, it was neither beauty nor impact, rather simply the shock of seeing her made

Byron forget, momentarily, how to take in air. So, I repeat, she was breathtaking. She was clearly a student of the history of red roses as a form of greeting, because in homage to the Neanderthal that first began the tradition, she was dressed in 100% leopard skin. Leopard skin top and skirt, both worn just a bit tighter than most leopards wear it. Byron was reminded of what PG Wodehouse had once said, it was as if she had been poured into her dress and someone had forgotten to say when. To make the ensemble complete, she touted a small leopard-skin purse and had 6-inch heels on with a leopard skin print along the heel. The lipstick was brighter red than the rose and the only thing larger than her persona was her hair.

Catching his breath, he quickly realized she had not noticed him yet. If he acted quickly, he could hide his rose and avoid a meeting that was sure to be as awkward as her skirt was short. But as his hand moved to the rose, she noticed him, made eye contact, smiled, and began heading his way.

As soon as she got within ten feet she opened up with a voice as big as her hair.

"So, you're my mystery man."

Byron nodded and reached out his hand to shake hers.

"Shake hands? I don't think so," she said, absolutely bubbling over. She then grabbed Byron, pulled him in for a hug, then moving her hands onto the back of his head, turned it to her and kissed him square on the lips. Again, breathing stopped. Finally, she released him and as he gasped for air, she said, "That is how you say hello."

"Well, Jennifer," Byron said, trying to get his bearings.

"Call me, Jen, or Honey Boo, if you'd rather," she said as she raised her eyebrows.

"Okay, Jen." He was going to say "nice to meet you" but had always been a poor liar, so changed it to, "Thanks for coming. My name is Byron."

"I love it," she jumped in before he could continue. "When I was a little girl, I dreamed of marrying a Byron, or was it Brian, no Ryan. But pretty close right, isn't that amazing!" Byron wasn't sure how to answer, and luckily while he puzzled on what to say, she asked, "Byron what?"

At this moment Byron had instantaneous thought. He did not want to tell her his last name. His desire that she have any ability to ever find him again was zero. The sooner he found himself under a sign that read *Exit,* the better. The second thought related to never seeing her again was that now that he was past the ambiance that was Jen, Honey Boo-boo, he had a strange feeling that this wasn't the first time he had seen her, but how he could have forgotten the encounter was beyond him.

"Hello? Byron, you there?" Clearly his thinking was too slow for her. "And people call *me* a ditz," she continued.

"Oh, sorry, have we met before? For some reason you look familiar."

"I don't remember meeting you before, and most people find me impossible to forget."

"I can see that," Byron agreed.

"So, Byron what is your last name?"

"Oh . . . uh . . . " Torn between lying and trying to come up with an excuse, he said, "Shouldn't we get to know each . . . Smith."

"Jen Smith. It is perfect. I never thought my name would be Jen Smith. I mean, I love it, but what are the chances I'd get someone with the name Smith?" At first Byron thought the question was hypothetical, but the blank look she continued to give was clearly wanting an answer.

"Actually, relative to other names, quite high, I think." Figuring he wasn't going to get out of a meal with Jen, he decided they better get started. So, before she could ask another question, he said, "Should we get something to eat?"

"Sounds great, do they have vegan or paleo here?"

"I'm not sure, you'll have to ask."

"I can't stand the thought of using animals for food. Except cows. And fish. See, I hate cows, and fish don't really count. But real animals, I love them. That is why I had my purse made with real fur, to always keep animals close to me. And paleo, I don't really know what it is, but I read that it's really changing the way people diet and I want to get on board."

Unable to commit on that sentiment, Byron ushered her to the counter, relieved his choice of fast casual would limit the length of this conversation. After a long discussion between Jen and the cashier on whether or not whipped cream was part of the paleo diet (she decided that it must be once she figured out it was a cow product), they sat down and began to work on their crepes.

Byron began strategizing how to let her down. But he also didn't want to be too abrupt or rude, so decided he better ask a few questions. Maybe one would lead to a good reason, beyond the obvious, why this wouldn't work.

"So, Jen, have you ever been married?"

She smiled and laughed. "Is this a trick question? I read the ad, no previous marriages. And I have not been, as long as you don't count the annulments, and the law doesn't count them, so I don't think it would be fair if you did."

"The annulments?" questioned Byron.

"Well first, turns out you can't marry your cousin, at least not when I tried. But the next time, on our wedding night, I found out he volunteered at kids' classes and hospitals and things as a clown, and I was like 'I don't think so, I'm not going to be married to no clown! Beam me up, Scotty. I'm out of here.' I should have asked my nephew how he met him when he set me up."

Suddenly it hit Byron. It was her reference to "beam me up Scotty." "You are Star Queen, you sent me two emails?"

She laughed. "No silly, I did not send you an email as Star Queen. My Star Trek-loving, alter ego is Star Jewell."

Byron waited for a minute, assuming she would elaborate on why the two emails, but since the question was about *Star Queen* she felt like the issue had been fully addressed.

"Okay, you sent me an email as 'Star Jewel.' Why did you send me two emails?"

"In case you weren't into Star Trek. Duh. Looks like it worked," she said with a wink.

"Star, Jen, Boo-boo," he rattled off before he got to the point, "this isn't going to work, I'm sorry."

"Wait! Are you breaking off our engagement?" she said loud enough that the fellow patrons began to listen.

Byron was not sure what to say but finally came up with, "We are not engaged."

She opened her mouth in shock and for a moment was speechless, as tears began to drip down her face. It was clear at this moment she was winning this case in the court of public opinion, and Byron heard someone from a nearby table mutter, "What a jerk."

After a few gasps of shock from Jen, she finally pulled her strength together and in her most powerful voice said, "Not engaged, huh, well that is rich, take this," as she smashed a half-eaten crepe with an excessive amount of strawberry syrup and whipped cream into his face. With syrup dripping down his shirt and onto the floor, Jen walked out to the cheers of the nearby diners.

Chapter 5

The Proposal

Byron found himself now with too much time and yet not enough. The entire episode with Jen had taken less than one hour, now he had over an hour before his next date, Nuts Julie. It was at a little panini shop on the other end of the casino. An hour is a long time to walk around a casino, especially when you don't gamble, even when accounting for the time he would need to spend in the bathroom trying to get strawberry syrup off his face and clothes. However, it was not long enough for him to go home and change his clothes, something he desperately wished he could do. He took some comfort that paninis, by nature, were much less messy when tossed at someone than crepes. One possibility was that Nuts Julie was simply Jen's third email to him. Yet, if it failed to be Jen's other alter ego, then what would Nuts Julie think of him showing up to meet her for the first time in a badly stained outfit?

He walked into the restroom and did an inventory of how truly bad it was. Wearing his favorite tie had clearly been a mistake and its light blue stripes were now a blotchy purple. The pink shirt absorbed the red syrup fairly well, but the outline of the stain was clearly visible. The rose was limp and crusted with dried whipped cream. Trying to remove it only led to the loss of pedals, and he quickly resolved that if he were to have any rose left, he better leave well enough alone.

At five minutes to 1:00, he started the trek to Café Bellagio, his lunch spot. Within minutes he had arrived and the first thing he noticed was a girl with a rose, but two things made him think this was not his date. For one, the rose was pink, and two, she looked normal. Normal didn't bother him but after Jen he thought his chances at completely normal was beyond the realm of possibility.

The normal girl with the pink rose kept glancing over at him but never got up. He kept watching for a red rose to walk in. After five minutes or so she walked over, "Excuse me are you waiting for someone?"

"Yes, I am looking for a Julie."

"I'm Julie."

"Oh sorry, I didn't think it was you."

"You didn't see the rose?" she said, pointing at it for emphasis.

"It's pink," Byron said.

"You are very perceptive," she said. "What's wrong with pink?"

"I guess, I expected red."

She paused, giving him time to explain himself, but since he didn't seem to feel obliged to, she continued with the question that was the obvious follow up, "Why?"

"Didn't I say, 'wear a red rose'?"

"Nope."

Both wanted to pull out the email and prove they were correct but, after a pause, realized there was little point, and moved on.

Julie, now seeing up close what was left of Byron's rose, asked, "Is yours frosted?"

This forced Byron to look down at his rose and he was reminded that when it came to the quality of roses, he was not on the moral high ground. "Yes, it is frosted . . . with whipped cream." He let the answer stand and she hardly knew what to say, it was clear she wanted the rest of the story. "I will simply say," he continued, "my last meeting didn't go so hot."

Julie tried not to, but a slight chuckle escaped her. "I'm sorry, but I have to hear this," she said, pulling up a chair and sitting down.

There was something about the way she spoke that calmed Byron and he decided to tell all, sparing no detail. Julie listened attentively right up to where he told her of being splattered with crepes. It was at this moment she interrupted their laughs with, "I am so glad to hear it!"

"Well, I'm glad it made you happy, it didn't warm my heart."

"No, it's just that your clothes had me a bit worried. I mean, I was nervous before I saw you that you would weigh 300 pounds or be unable to dress yourself, and you looked surprisingly normal except for the stains, and I thought, 'That's it, he never changes his clothes, probably hasn't showered since Bush was in the White House.' So, I am happy that it was simply a prospective bride showering you with breakfast."

"Well, I hope you don't plan to follow suit."

"Okay, Mr. Smith," she mockingly referred to the false name he had given to Jen, "Do I get to know your real name?"

"Sure, Lewis. Byron Lewis."

"That's not too bad, I prefer Smith, but what are you going to do?"

"Well, shall we go order?" Byron suggested.

"Do you know if they have any paleo, vegan food with whipped cream?" They both laughed as they approached the counter to order.

Once they had their food and sat down to eat, Julie asked the first question. "Byron, tell me honestly, why are you doing this? No offense, but it is way beyond weird."

"I think you called it 'nuts' in the email."

"Exactly, nuts. So why?"

"You can keep a secret?"

"Mums the word."

"I am a marriage counselor," Byron said.

"Oh, I see," she said, holding in a chuckle. "People are getting sick of taking advice from a novice. Wait, less than a novice. A novice has at least a little experience, you have none."

"Thank you. I think you get the idea."

"So, why not find a girl and get married the old-fashioned way?"

"I always planned on dating and getting married, but I was busy and being single has been working fine for me. I mean, except for what others think. But I am fine being single and am fine staying single the rest of my life. Well, single, but kind of married, on paper at least. You know, as I outlined in the ad."

"I totally understand, what is wrong with being single? People think I sit home at night crying or something. Being single works for me too."

"All right, my turn. Why did you apply to the ad?"

"Two reasons. One, my mother. Someday, I will be sitting over her deathbed, weeping, telling her I love her, and she will look into my eyes and say, 'Are you dating anyone? When are you going to get married?' I say that, but it really isn't how it would be because she will simply refuse to die until I have sworn matrimony. And two, I am so sick of getting set up, or having to avoid strange men who want to date me."

It was her time to play story time and she began to tell all about Larry at her office and his most recent push to get a date to the Garth Brooks concert. She closed with, "I would love for Larry to walk into my office, see a photo of me in my wedding dress, and for the first time see his mouth open and no words come out."

"I love it," he responded. The more she went on, the more he felt like this was the girl for him. Truly a perfect match, a win-win. She needed to be married without being married and so did he. So, he decided to put it out there, "I don't want to rush things, but given what you said, I think this could work."

"What are you saying?"

"I guess, I'm asking you to marry me?"

"Oh, that's cute . . . try again."

He stared blankly. "Oh, I got it. Julie." Then he stopped. "What is your last name?"

"Smith."

"Really?"

"Yup, as you told good old Jen, it's not that uncommon."

"Well then, Julie Smith, will you marry me?"

"Sure."

Chapter 6

Competition

M any men may have wanted a more confident answer to, "Will you marry me?", than, "sure," but it was good enough for Byron.

"Great. This is Vegas, do you prefer the Justice of the Peace, drive thru chapel, or wee little chapel on the strip?"

Without a pause, came the confident reply, "St. Mark's." No matter what the circumstances were, she wanted a real wedding.

"St. Mark's? A church?"

"Yes, a church."

"Would a church do a wedding without notice?"

"We're not getting married today."

Byron was confused; it seemed to be a beautiful day. Of all days, he didn't see what made this one less worthy than any other. "What's wrong with today?" This process of finding a bride had already taken several days, and he didn't care to have it drag on forever.

"Byron, one of the major reasons I'm doing this is to appease my mother. And I will admit, I don't see her all that often, only once every few years, but I have a feeling she will be a little upset if she finds out I didn't invite her to my wedding."

"I guess that makes sense." He contemplated the situation and decided to give in. "Okay, we can do it next week if that works better."

"Not next week, maybe, six months from now."

"Six months?" Why would they possibly wait six months!? "Why six months?" Byron asked.

"I don't want my parents and others to think I'm rushing into it. Plus, we need to plan it."

"Plan?"

"You really are a novice at this wedding thing."

"If you really need time to do a few things, I understand. We can wait a month."

"Three months at a minimum."

"I'm reasonable, six weeks."

"Do you realize how busy we will be if we try to do this in six weeks?" Julie asked.

Secretly, he thought this couldn't take longer than a few minutes of planning but decided not to bring that up right now and instead said, "I love being busy."

"Okay, six weeks from today it is."

"Great. Where is this church of yours?"

"Southwest part of town. The pastor will want to meet with us."

Byron clenched his teeth. While he grimaced, she continued. "If we are going to do this in six weeks, we had better get photos for the invitation tomorrow."

"Wait a minute. Why would we want photos, or need invitations?"

"Calm down, Byron." Her tone did not impress Byron, who thought that she should wait at least until they were married before she started talking down to him. "You want to pass this off as the real deal, don't you? Wouldn't it be more convincing if you had a picture of me and you on your desk?"

She was right, but that didn't mean he was going to be happy about it. If he had realized photos would have been part of the deal, he would have thought a bit more about putting that ad in the paper. "Okay, so let's sit down and figure a bit of this out." So that's exactly what they did. It was 2:50 before Byron realized it. "Holy cow, it's almost three. I need to get over to Paris."

"Quite the world traveler, huh."

"No, Paris hotel across the street, for my next . . . well . . . appointment."

"How many of these *appointments* do you have today?" Julie asked.

"She's the last one."

"You're going to meet with her after you proposed to me?"

"Well, at this point, I'm not sure I have much of an option. I can't stand her up. That would be rude."

"Just call her."

"I don't have her number. Say, why don't you come with me? I can quickly tell her it's off and then we can go get rings while we work out all the details."

"Sounds good. I know it's probably wrong, but I'm rather anxious to see her. I mean, what kind of a wacko is willing to get married based on an ad in the paper? Besides you and me, of course. What's her name?"

"Julie."

"Another nuts Julie."

"No, you're Nuts Julie. She's just Julie."

She glared at the back of his head as she followed him out the door.

There are few walks more famous or more unique than the walk from the Bellagio to the Paris Casino on the Strip in Las Vegas. And while neither mentioned it, both felt a small amount of regret and significant irony that their first walk as an engaged couple would be such a blur. They blurred through the casino, past the beautiful conservatory in the Bellagio, through the magnificent entrance, and past the world-famous fountains. Once they were out in front of the walkway, the crowds grew dense, and you couldn't toss a brick in any direction without hitting a street performer dressed as Buzz Lightyear, Darth Vader, or Batman, all ready to be in your next selfie for a small fee. Dashing across the busy street, they entered the Paris Casino. After passing a few slot machines, they took the elevator up to the one-third scale Eiffel tower to the restaurant and his waiting, final appointment.

Despite their rush, they approached the front desk at 3:07. "Can I help you?" The greeter behind the front desk said. Looking towards the dining area Byron noticed some of the tables, and spotted a red rose and knew it must be Julie.

"I am here to meet someone."

"Yes, sir, whom are you here to meet?"

"I think I see her back there, but just a second." He turned to Julie, "Okay, Julie, you stay here and I'll go tell her that it's off."

"That's disappointing." Julie said with a bit of a frown.

"What is?"

"She looks rather likeable." I kind of wanted to see someone like that Jen you described earlier. Not to mention, it'd be fun to see her throw her plate at you."

"I hope to be out of here before she has a plate of food to throw. Wish me luck."

"I'll be watching."

The host took him to his seat. When he had taken the job as host at the Paris hotel, he had assumed that each night would be full of exciting situations. A man showing up to meet one woman with another woman in the lobby was something he figured would be as commonplace as peanut butter and jelly, and that is saying something given that his last name was Smucker. But in this hope, he was greatly disappointed. Life, even on the strip, was not as exciting as advertised. While he desperately wanted to have thrilling tales of high rollers letting hundred-dollar bills fall from their pockets while a train of show girls followed behind, most of his clients were simply regular couples coming for a nice meal. Byron with one woman waiting at the table and one watching from yonder lobby was of keen interest to him, and while he didn't know the back story, he was convinced it was about to come out as long as he stayed within ear shot. "Here you are, sir," he said, pulling out the chair across the rose-adorned guest.

"Thank you," Byron said, but it was a lie. He had no desire to take a seat and was not thankful for this gesture. His plan had been to approach her from one side of the table, tell her he couldn't stay as he lapped around the table and then put a little breeze in her hair from his draft as he headed back towards the door. But now with the host holding the chair for him, he was rather obliged to take a seat. "Are you Julie?"

She grinned from ear to ear. "I am, and you must be my mystery man or a secret liaison that is going to drive me in a limo to a secret location where there's a man behind a desk,"

"Actually," Byron interrupted, but unsuccessfully.

"Of course, I won't be able to see him because he's turned around in a big chair. I turn back to the man that brought me, but the door shuts and I am locked in the room with the man in the big chair. Silence sets over us as he allows the fear inside me to grow. Finally, when the tension has grown to almost the point of bursting, he will call out the single deep syllable, 'Julie.'"

Byron wanted to point out that "Julie" was two syllables, but the storyteller was not allowing interruptions. "The voice will sound vaguely familiar, but could it be? While I'm torn with thoughts of the past, the voice will continue, 'Julie, I have searched the world over and now you can finally be mine.' Then I will be sure and will run to him. As he spins around in the chair, I will call out, 'Billy, I knew you would find me. No matter how lonely or far I was, I knew you would come.'"

At this point, she was so into the story that Byron was fairly sure if he walked out right now she might not notice, and debated doing it.

"We then passionately kiss and sink into this large chair, which is big, but far too small for both of us, but that is fine with me. And then . . . " She snapped out of it as she saw Byron and the host staring at her. "So, are you my mystery man?"

"I guess so . . . who's Billy?"

"I'd rather not talk about Billy."

"Okay." By time time, he had planned to say that he couldn't stay but the story of the liaisons, limos, and Billy had thrown him off a bit. Trying to think of a good way to transition from, yes, I am the mystery man to, now I need to mysteriously disappear was bothering him, but he figured that conversation would be easier without the presence of this very attentive host who was still standing by his side. "Thank you again . . . Kevin," he said, noting the name tag. "I think we're good for now."

"I would like to introduce you to your waiter. He will be here momentarily." He said this while standing at perfect attention staring directly forward. Clearly the host had no intention of leaving in the immediate future.

Byron looked back towards the lobby and saw Julie watching his poor performance. "So, there is no limo or man behind the desk, but I do need . . . "

He was about to say, " . . . to go" but Julie again interrupted, "Actually that is really good. When I answered this thing, I thought, 'I bet that this guy is four-hundred pounds or like seventy-five or something, but you look great. I mean, you could lose a few pounds, but who couldn't? Overall, you are like an eight, okay, maybe a seven. Not that looks are everything, mind you, but it is nice to enjoy that person you need to wake up to every morning. I remember, I used to wake up every morning and look at my dog. And I would say you are somewhat of an improv—"

"Listen, Julie, I can't stay. Something has come up and I have to go." Boy, did that feel good. He had done it. He scooted his chair back as the beginning of his leaving motion.

"Oh, no. Did someone die?" Julie asked in shock and seriousness.

"No, nothing that serious but I do have to leave. I am so sorry you came all this way, but I must go." Byron again continued his motions of leaving, almost forgetting the host he was about to run into.

"Okay, I understand." Byron was so relieved to be done with that. "So, when do you want to reschedule?"

Reschedule? Oh no, she wasn't getting it. Byron had always thought finding people to date would be hard, now he saw why he never started. It wasn't finding people that was hard, it was getting rid of them. He didn't know what to say but decided to be honest without any elaboration. At some point, one might expect him to realize that strategy didn't work, but nonetheless, he stuck to it. "Julie, there is no need to reschedule." There was no intention for the words to come off harsh but as soon as they left his mouth, he could tell that is exactly how it came off.

Tears began to well up in Julie's eyes. "Wait a minute."

Byron halted in place half-standing and only inches from the still frozen host whose only movement was the edge of his lips that couldn't help but begin to smile.

Exasperation filled her voice, "You send me an email saying you want to meet me, because you need a wife, practically proposing to me, and then I drive clear across town fighting the crazy traffic through the strip and you take one look at me and say it's over. Clearly, you think looks are nice too, but mine aren't nice enough for you, and you can't even take the time to inconvenience yourself enough to sit down and eat with me, you're no better than Billy."

Byron decided to ignore the reference to Billy. "It's not your looks Julie."

"What then? What has come up? Why don't you want to reschedule?"

What he had been avoiding from the get go, the truth, now seemed his only solution. "I decided on another girl and didn't have time to cancel, so I thought I'd better let you know rather than leave you hanging."

"You decided before you even met me? That doesn't seem very fair."

Byron was not sure what to say. Fairness had not been on his mind when he had proposed to Julie, and in his defense, he kind of thought past case law may be in his favor in this regard. He was not a master of jurisprudence but he did know that all is fair in love and war. And while his case may be a stretch to be called love, he thought a jury would buy it. However, how to articulate this at that moment didn't come readily to him, he was just wondering what would Billy do? When she saved him the trouble by continuing.

"Well fine. Can I at least get my dinner? You did drag me all this way."

"Um . . . I um . . . " Byron stammered when unsure of what to do, "See, it turns out that she's out front, and I should really . . . "

"She is here? Great! I would like to meet her. Have her come on back."

Byron had been in counseling long enough to know that this was a bad idea, but before he could decline, the ever-attentive host, Kevin, said, "I will get her," and was off with more alacrity than he had ever performed any task to date in his life.

Seconds later, there they all were: Julie, Julie, Byron, and of course, the ever-specious host, Kevin. Julie, Byron's first date, spoke as she approached. "So, Byron, we have decided to stay?"

Julie #2 jumped in, which was good, because Byron didn't know what to say, "Byron was good enough to at least stay for dinner, given that I came all this way and I so wanted to meet you."

"Oh, good . . . this should be nice," Julie said, half under her breath, as she grabbed a chair which allowed Byron to sit as well.

Again, silence fell on the group and it was the silence's presence that made the presence of the host, still standing at attention, stand out. Byron was not happy with the growing number at the table and decided he better get rid of someone, unfortunately for the host, he was the easiest target. "Can we all get a glass of water?"

"No, I'll have a glass of your Haynes Old Block, Pinot Noir. Actually, go ahead and bring us a bottle," Julie #2 said with a smile.

Byron knew that divorce was expensive; he regularly said so as an incentive for couples to continue with his services. He was now worried that he was about to get a taste of how expensive break ups could be.

The host wished to protest but could see the manager headed their way and a line back at the front door, so, as much as he wished to see this play out, he was forced to depart.

As soon as he left, #2 started in. Looking to Julie #1, she said, "It's good to meet you. What's your name?"

"Julie."

"Well, isn't that nice. It seems our friend Byron here has a thing for Julies. See, I'm named Julie as well."

"I know," #1 admitted.

"You know," she said, looking at Byron, "So, what else did Byron tell you about me?"

"That was it." Julie said in all honesty.

Byron was a bit defensive at this point. After all, when you're running a "find a bride" advertisement scheme, you don't want people to think you're careless with participants' privacy. "What else could I tell her, that is all I knew."

"That's true," #2 pounced, "but it was enough to know you wanted her over me. You must have loved her name more. Oh wait, it's the same name."

Byron was getting happier by the second that he hadn't picked #2. "I know you are upset, but let's try to stay calm."

"Okay." She took a deep breath. "I can stay calm. So, when is the big day?"

Byron didn't want to answer but decided they couldn't sit in silence. "We're looking at six weeks from now."

It is amazing how our tone can express so much more than our words. Byron had stated a brief factual sentence but how he said it and how he looked at Julie, that is #1, is what told Julie, that is #2, that six weeks was not what Byron had in mind. This is the exact opening that #2 had been hoping would show, but before she could exploit it, the waiter showed up with water and her very pricey bottle of wine.

"What can I get for you?"

Byron was ready and, hoping to minimize the damage, quickly ordered the cheapest meal on the menu. Julie #1 followed suit with a similarly priced item. Byron's admiration for this woman was growing. Then came #2, and, much to his surprise, she said, "I'll have the same." Byron sat relieved, maybe the damage would not be as bad as he thought.

"Why wait?" She began to go for the weakness. "What's wrong with today?" #2 asked as the waiter walked away.

Byron wanted to jump up and say, "Exactly what I said," but, in what can only be considered a miracle, he thought for a moment before he spoke. Saving his engagement, he said, "We feel it would be good to wait, to invite our families and do other important marriage things."

This was 100% the right answer but 0% believable. #2 could tell she was heading in the right vein and pressed further. "You know I wouldn't need to wait for my family to come."

No one responded. "So, did you guys talk turkey?" While turkey was consumed at his earlier lunch, he was fairly confident that was not what #2 was talking about, but he wasn't sure what she was talking about. Everyone present had a confused look on their face except Kevin; he had come back and was again standing by the side of the table, a smile of feigned disinterest and glee on his face as Julie #2 continued, "I mean did Julie agree to the $500 a month that you had in your ad?"

The question seemed personal and inappropriate, but then again, there was nothing appropriate or normal about their entire situation. "We have not discussed that yet," Byron admitted.

"What if she wants more?" #2 asked.

Byron now noted the smiling host by his side. "What are you doing here?"

"I came by to ensure that everything is meeting your satisfaction," came the perfectly composed reply.

Byron was about to tell him to take a hike, but #1 spoke up and said to #2, "Have you forgotten that I am right here. Not that it is any of your business, but I don't plan to ask for more."

#2 looked right at Byron and said, "I'll take half."

Byron couldn't believe this. It was absurd and ridiculous, but suddenly he paused, forgetting about Kevin, he wondered if he wasn't being too hasty. Either woman he would rarely see, and #2 was willing to marry today and for half price. Not only that, she probably wouldn't require him to sit for photos. For a moment he thought about breaking off his engagement with #1, but only for a moment. After all, a jerk is still a jerk, even at half price.

"Listen, Julie," he said, looking directly at #2. "This is not a debate. I'm going to marry Julie." Then realizing this may not be as clear as it should be, he clarified, "This Julie." He pointed to make sure everyone understood. And then turning to Kevin said, "We will pay for the food now and take ours to go."

Julie #1 was impressed. Byron may not be a knight in shining armor, but a man smart enough to run away when needed might live longer anyway.

With victory on his mind, he stood, taking Julie's hand. "We will pay at the front desk," he told Kevin.

But before the victory went too far to his head, #2 turned to Kevin and said, "Before you ring him up, you might want to note that I'll be changing my order to the filet mignon and lobster tail, oh, and let me see that wine list again."

Chapter 7

Visiting the Priest

As much as Byron hated to admit it, Julie was right. There was a lot to plan for the wedding. For the next few weeks, he had to order a tux, go get rings, and send out invitations. And there would have been more if he hadn't talked her out of a reception. The idea of having to talk to family for more than the two seconds before the ceremony, made him ill, and he was glad she was willing to see his side on this one.

Julie wouldn't have to have any awkward moments with his side because Julie sent out far more invitations than he had. He hadn't planned on inviting anyone, but with Julie sending out close to 100 invitations, he thought he'd better send out a few. Deep down, he hoped this particular Lutheran Church didn't stick too rigidly to the old tradition of his family on one side and hers on the other. It would be a bit awkward when they have standing room only on her side and his side being his lone dad. While he had sent out a few invitations, he thought the only person who would show up would be his dad. His dad had always loved him but their conversations since his mother died had become shorter and shorter, neither were really into chatting on the phone. But while he worried a little about how his father would react, today was the day that an encounter with a different father was on his mind, one he feared far more than the encounter with his own father. It was Father Young, the local priest at the Lutheran church.

Byron didn't think it was common for priests or pastors, or whatever you call them, to go by father in the Lutheran church, assuming that was more a Catholic thing. But common or not, Julie assured him that he went by Father Young. Supposedly, he came from a long line of Episcopal Priests, and while the religion didn't stick, the name did.

So, with no shortage of fear, he parked his car in the parking lot of St. Mark's Lutheran church. The light blue Toyota Prius already in the parking lot announced to him that Julie had beaten him. A smile ran over his face as he saw it. She would give him a hard time about arriving first, even though he was on time, but he was looking forward to that. He liked her subtle and almost flirtatious jabs. In fact, while he was anxious for this whole wedding thing to be in the rear-view mirror, his one regret was that it would end his regular interaction with Julie. He hated pictures, invitations, shopping, and planning, but doing it with Julie made it bearable. If he were honest, more than bearable, he looked forward to seeing her.

But the arrangement was clear. He had told her originally there wouldn't be contact after the wedding and she clearly agreed. After all, she hadn't said anything to let him think she wanted anything else. They would do what was necessary. He knew there would be moments when people would ask where she was, and he figured she would have to make excuses for him too. For a moment, he wondered if this idea of never contacting one another was going too far. No, he had agreed to this arrangement and he'd stick to it.

"Hey, Julie," he said as he approached the front doors where she stood. She looked down at her watch, faking irritation. "Oh, so what time does your watch say?" Byron asked, clearly trying to rub in that he was indeed on time.

"It says you are late."

"You need a new watch."

"I thought I explained this to you, if you aren't ten minutes early, you're late."

"No, the first time you said five minutes and last time when you showed up barely on time, the topic didn't come up at all."

"It's a rule with varied application, and clearly I alone know how to properly apply it. For example, one should always arrive early so they don't leave their bride standing at the front door of the chapel. Doing so is exceptionally risky. She may get bored and pick up another one of her many suitors who happen to walk by."

"A very risky situation indeed. Do your suitors regularly pass by this thoroughfare of pedestrian traffic?" Byron said, motioning to the totally deserted sidewalk in front of the church.

Julie laughed lightly as she said, "Well, we better go in before you make us late because I had to explain everyday decorum to you."

As they entered the church, Byron's light mood ended, and he felt a heavy burden on his shoulder. The church was beautiful. It was an older church and was cathedral-esque in its grandeur. The wood pews looked newly polished as the sun flooded through the stained glass. This church felt like the real deal. There was a reverence in the building and the fact that this felt like a real church and a great place to connect with God, made Byron feel uneasy. Somehow, being married in the eyes of the guy running the drive thru wedding chapel on the strip didn't seem wrong in the slightest but saying "I do" in front of a priest in this edifice under the circumstances did not sit well with him.

Looking closer at some of the stained glass, he noted that one window depicted the story of someone getting married. The first window showed a rather dark and somewhat disappointing wedding. Then it showed the young man going back to work. The artist had worked extra hard to make the work appear to be arduous and painful. Well, after a few more depictions of backbreaking labor, there was another wedding with the same man and a different bride that appeared much brighter and overall more joyful then the first. Byron knew the place was famous for weddings but could not figure out why any chapel would have such a story in stained glass. It appeared either the focus was "marriage is nothing but painful work," or "don't worry, your next marriage will make you happy." While he was puzzling over the stained glass, Julie had already headed for the priest office. Finding that Byron had failed to follow, she went back, grabbed him by the arm, and pulled him and in the right direction.

They opened a door, and it took them from the beautiful chapel to a rather normal looking office. "Hello. So good to see you," said a nice-looking middle-aged man behind the desk. "Come in."

Byron was a bit surprised. When he thought of meeting with a priest, he thought of sitting down in the pews with a man in a large robe or toga or something. This guy simply had on a nice shirt and tie. In fact, he was dressed a lot like Byron. The priest also seemed too young. Despite his name being Father Young, Byron had imagined someone the opposite. At some point in his life, he got the image of a priest being old and grizzled. Perhaps a bit senile, interspersed with moments of deep insight. And the image stuck. He realized now this didn't make much sense.

"So, this must be Byron," the priest said, shaking Byron's hand. It was clear he must know Julie. Byron didn't even realize that this was her church. He figured she just picked it because it looked nice. "Well, it's a pleasure to meet you, Byron. I'm Father Young," the priest said.

"Good to meet you," Byron said.

"Have a seat," Father Young said as he went back behind the desk. "So, you two want to get married. I think that is wonderful. How long have you two been dating?" Byron had mostly thought this would be a logistical meeting. You know the "I stand here, you stand there, you say this, I say this and it will cost X." Even this made him uncomfortable, but if he had he figured there were to be deep, piercing, personal questions like, "How long have you been dating?" he would have prepared some evasive answers. Given his lack of preparation and since Julie knew the Father, he thought he would just let her answer. After a long pause it was clear Julie had a similar strategy.

Finally, Byron looked at Julie and said, "How long has it been?"

Julie, clearly not in the habit of lying to clergy, simply said, "I hardly remember. It's gone by so quick."

Father waited, clearly expecting they would continue with something like, "Well, let's see, it was before you bought the new car and that was a year ago . . ." but Julie and Byron had technically answered the question and weren't volunteering anything else until another one was asked.

"Well, how did you meet?"

Boy, those priests sure know how to get to the heart of a subject. Byron had no idea what to say now. It's not that a flat-out lie didn't sound good to him, but he didn't know if Julie wanted to lie to her priest, so he decided if a tactic worked once, why not try it again? "How did we meet?" he questioned turning to Julie.

She smiled at him, the kind of smile that did not leave you feeling all warm and fuzzy. "Remember we ran into each other at that little panini shop at the Bellagio," she said with the perfect hint of "I can't believe you forgot our anniversary" in her voice to come off as believable. Boy was she good at this, and it was sure coming in handy now, however he was wondering if he could ever truly trust someone this good at half-truths.

"Oh, that's right, how could I forget. I was getting ready to do some interviews for work and we just started talking. We enjoyed each other's company so much, I cancelled my next interview and we went out to dinner," he said, doing his best to sound hopelessly in love. With a little encouragement from Julie, he was getting the hang of this. Their dating experience was beginning to sound, not half bad.

"So, Byron, what do you do for a living?"

Here, Byron had little to hide, but since meeting Julie, he had determined not to hear any more lectures about how only married people really know about marriage, and, knowing that telling Father Young he was a marriage counselor would cause that, he simply said. "I am a counselor."

"At a school?" Father Young replied.

"No, I have my own practice." Byron said trying to keep it as simple as possible.

"What type of counseling?"

"People, mostly." Byron wished he had left off mostly, but it had the desired effect and there were no more questions about his work.

"Byron." Father leaned forward and his face grew somber. "What church do you belong to?"

"Oh, well I haven't really attended church in years. I don't really belong to any church."

"Do you see God as an important part of your future marriage with Julie?"

Oh, boy, how do you give a half-truth answer to a yes or no question? Not only that, Byron knew the statistics. He was always encouraging couples to be united in faith or come to agreement on where they stood religiously. It helps marriages, but their marriage was different. He didn't want a marriage in the eyes of God, just in the eyes of those around him. If only he'd persuaded Julie to go with that drive-thru chapel.

Fortunately, however, he had seen hundreds of men just like him squirm under difficult questions when he was on the other side of the desk, and if there was one thing men were good at when under pressure, it was acting dumb.

"I just haven't really thought about it before."

Byron knew this would elicit a speech from Father Young, but sitting and taking a speech was a lot easier than coming up with answers to questions. Father Young was a very good speaker, and Byron agreed, in principle at least, with everything he said in his rather lengthy speech on God and marriage.

After his speech, he started another speech about how running a church was expensive. Byron was confused, at first, why this was part of the marriage speech, but realized he was preparing to tell Byron that the marriage would not be free. This was a speech Byron felt no need to make Father Young go through the pain of giving, because it was obvious that while Father Young enjoyed delivering the speech on marriage, he did not enjoy the follow up speech on money.

"Father Young, we plan on paying for the opportunity to marry here," Byron interrupted the speech.

Father Young sighed and sat back in his chair. Then followed it with, "We welcome any donation, but the ceremony does cost us a certain amount." Father Young relayed the cost and Byron assured him that he was happy to pay. Byron was pleased to pay him for the service. Byron's guilt had been building, but somehow, paying Father Young eased it some.

Byron, having passed the inquisition, and Father Young, having been assured they would pay, both were much calmer than when they began. All three went out to see the chapel and work out a few logistics for the big day.

"I'm open until my dress appointment in a few hours, do you want to grab something to eat?" Julie said as they walked out of the chapel.

"You bet."

"I can let you see some pictures of the floral arrangements I picked out."

"Actually, I just remembered, I have a hair appointment," Byron said.

"Good, that mop needs a lot of work before the wedding."

"It was a joke."

"So was mine, I like your mop. So, do you want to come up with a fake appointment or join me for lunch?"

"Lunch would be great. Even if I have to look at pictures of flowers."

"Then hop in. I'll bring you back to your car after," Julie said.

"Byron, why did you become a marriage counselor in the first place," Julie asked once they had agreed upon a soup and salad place they both loved and pulled into traffic.

"My parents were the main reason, I wanted to help people have what they had."

"Have you?"

"Have I what?" Byron responded.

"Helped people find what your parents had?"

There was a significant pause. "I hope so. I try, but I guess I haven't sat back and took stock in a while. Why did you become an engineer?"

"My reasons were much less noble than yours. I was good at math and engineers made good money." Julie said.

"Very practical, perfect for an engineer."

"I guess . . . "

"Julie watch out." Just then a car came blaring through the intersection in front of them. Julie slammed on her brake as she swerved into the lane next to her. The reaction was perfect and she only scratched the back end of the car that totally ignored her as it continued to fly down the street.

"Wasn't my light green?" Julie said. Trying to see the lights that she was now directly under.

"It was. That guy totally ran that red light." And as Byron said, it they understood why sirens could be heard and three seconds later officers followed the speeding vehicle, clearly in pursuit.

"I'm just glad no one was next to me," Julie said. Cars were now beginning to stack up in the intersection. And they all watched as Julie turned around and began to pull out of the way and into a parking lot.

"Julie, you were amazing. If you hadn't reacted so quickly, we would, well we probably wouldn't be walking upright right now," Byron said as she pulled into a parking stall. She didn't respond to Byron and, as he looked over, he could see why. Clearly the adrenaline had worn off and shock was taking its place. She was in the parking spot and just staring ahead, shaking slightly.

Byron got out of his door, went around and opened Julie's. "Are you okay Julie?"

She didn't respond for a moment, then said, "I guess."

"Hey Julie, why don't you lean your chair back." He spoke calm and slowly and she did as he instructed. "Close your eyes and allow your breathing to slow."

"Should we call the cops?" she said as she shook.

"We can call anyone we need to in a moment. First, we can take a moment and make sure you are okay. Allow your breathing to slow. We are both safe and you did exactly the right thing. You saved our lives. Focus on slowly taking in breath, one, two, three, four, five, six, hold and exhale, one, two, three, four, five, six." As Byron reached out and turned the car off, he could see her nerves starting to calm.

He sat quietly next to her for a few minutes before she said, "Thanks, I needed that, I think I was just going into a little shock."

"Understandable, given the circumstances."

"Do you do that in therapy sessions?"

He nodded.

"Well, you're very good at it," Julie said. "What should we do now?"

"I guess we should look at the damage and decide if you want to have your insurance fix it. If so, we should probably call the police and get a police report."

They walked around and saw a few black streaks on her white bumper. "I like them, they add character." They both laughed. "You still want lunch?"

"If you're up to it," Byron responded.

"I think that'd be good. But do you mind driving?"

"Not at all."

After a decent but uneventful lunch they headed back to the car. "Do you want me to drive again?"

"If you would."

"Do you want me to take you to your dress appointment?"

"Are you serious? You'd go to my dress appointment?"

"If you want me to. Being around others after a traumatic incident can be helpful."

"That is very good of you. But you're not supposed to see me in my dress until the big day."

"I said I'd give you a ride, I didn't say I'd come in. I have some podcasts I'd like to catch up on. I can wait in the car. It will be like being a teenager again."

"I still can't believe you are willing to do this for me, just sit and wait—but thanks," Julie said.

And sit and wait he did. He was still sitting and hour and a half later when she returned.

"Where to next?" Byron cheerfully said as she got back into the car.

"Wow! What service. Have you thought of being a professional chauffeur?"

"I don't like the hats they wear."

"Good point. But unfortunately, I've got nowhere else on the list, so back to the church lot to pick up your car."

"I can take you home."

"How would you get your car back?"

"I can get a taxi."

"No, go back to the church. I'm doing fine now and think I'm ready to get behind the wheel. Don't you councilors say when you fall off get right back up?" Julie asked.

"I have been known to say that."

"Good, then why don't you get out and let me play chauffeur for a bit," Julie said.

As they crossed around the car, Byron took a long look at his soon-to-be bride. He had thought she was beautiful from the moment he met her, but the more he got to know her the better and better looking she became.

Chapter 8

The Night before the Wedding

"So, you are at passenger pickup?" Byron asked.

"Ready and waiting," came the reply.

"I'll be there in two minutes."

Byron pulled into the passenger pickup lane amidst the blaring whistle that was being wielded by a man in a yellow vest. This man's sole job was to make sure no one stopped in passenger pickup long enough to pick up a passenger. While the yellow jacket used the weapon of a sharp whistle and loud voice, drivers employed a far more effective weapon, feigned ignorance. Step one was avoiding eye contact while crawling at 0.5 mph, hoping their brother, wife, niece, or business partner would emerge. But with the constant whistle and yelling, eye contact could only be avoided for so long and then it was time for step two. The classic, "who me?" look. "You were yelling and blowing your whistle at me?" The shocked look of bewilderment and forcing the yellow jacket to give the "yes, you, get moving" look back, buys you an extra 30–45 seconds. At that point, one is forced to move along. That is unless you are lucky enough for Yellow Jacket to turn their attention to the next car that is avoiding their eye contact. At which point, you can say, "Oh, I guess you weren't yelling at me." And go back to step one.

Byron noticed one particularly adept driver ahead. This driver feigned ignorance so well, one wondered if any feigning was involved.

There they sat parked in the passenger pickup line with no passenger in sight. The yellow jacket blew a loud whistle, then yelled, "Move along," while breathing in, a skill they must have learned as part of circular breathing training back when they were the first chair didgeridoo player. They then blew an even longer, louder whistle. The parked driver, sans passenger, sat acting totally oblivious—100% successful at the eye contact avoidance. With the trusty whistle and yell routine not producing satisfaction, the yellow jacket approached and knocked on the window. The driver debated feigning deafness but ultimately acknowledged the yellow jacket and the window began its descent.

"You can't park here. You need to keep moving."

A blank stare was the only reply.

"If your passenger is not here, you need to move along." This was followed by an arm motion meant to portray the movement the yellow jacket hoped to inspire.

Byron was wondering how much money the yellow jacket must be paid in order to show such dedication to the cause of proper traffic flow, when the driver finally responded. "Cómo?"

"You think, I believe, you don't speak English?" the yellow jacket protested.

"Qué?"

Just then, a lovely young woman ran up to the car, pulled open the back door and said, "Hey, Dad."

Embarrassment flushed over the drivers face.

The yellow jacket gave a world-class condescending stare, and the man chose to respond with the gas pedal, leaving the yellow jacket to turn his anger and whistle onto Byron. Luckily, weapons were useless because Byron had what he needed, a passenger. He was happy to avoid feigning ignorance or lack of ability to speak English and stepped out of the car turning to his passenger and said, "Hey, Dad." His dad gave a sincere smile as they got back into the car. It was the first time they'd been face to face in a long time.

Once back in the car, silence prevailed for a long time before Byron asked, "So, was the flight good?"

"Yeah, as good as a four-hour flight can be."

"So, how's the town?"

"Not much changes there. That's why I like it."

Silence again settled in. Both men loved each other but neither was much for expressing it. Lately, when in each other's presence they didn't say much of anything. And "lately" would only be an apt description if speaking in geologic times. Truthfully, they had only ever really reacted well when combined with the proper catalyst and that catalyst had always been Byron's mom. Somehow, she knew exactly how to keep the family properly mixed. And six years ago, when she passed away from cancer, the now small, two-person family fell apart.

Not due to any fighting or animosity, there was just no, well anything. Without his mother to play instigator, nothing got instigated. Byron's dad did call every year on Byron's birthday and said, "Well, Happy Birthday son." At that point the call became much like this ride from the airport: silent, with a small burst of superficial questions to avoid complete failure to interact.

Just such a burst started when dad asked, "So, everything ready for the big day?"

"Yeah. Julie's really done most of the planning and work."

"Makes sense . . . Not that you can't plan, but women . . ." He was about to say that they are better at these things, but just left the thought as incomplete as their conversation.

On the birthday call this was the part when one of them would say, "Well, better get going." But today, with both sitting in the car, they knew that any *going* was to be done together.

It was as he grabbed the suitcase from the trunk that he remembered the one thing he needed to ask his dad. The one thing he was solely in charge of.

"Oh Dad, did you bring the tux?"

"Sure did. Had it cleaned just before I came. This will be the first time it has been worn since Mom and I got married."

Byron could have done without the last line. It wasn't that he wasn't sentimental, he could be. But, so far he had done his best to separate real life family, marriage, and, indeed, love from the business transaction taking place in the morning. Exactly how far he tried to separate the two became clear to Julie three weeks earlier.

"You got your hundred invites, correct?" Julie has asked.

"Yup," Byron honestly responded.

"Have you sent them out? I was up the last two nights getting all mine in the mail."

"I handed some out."

"What do you mean, 'you handed some out?' Like you passed them out to some homeless as they walked by?"

"No. I gave a few out at work." And this he had done. His office only contained himself and his assistant Ms. Whitacker. So, she got one. But since he was anxious to have this connected with work, he gave out invites to anyone connected with his job: Dr. Morris and Dr. Reise, whom he both consulted with and referred patients to, each got one; the office manager who ran the building they leased space in; even the guy who owned the shop two doors down that he usually got lunch from got one, but that was it.

"What did you do with the rest?" Julie asked.

"Keepsakes?"

"Are you going to mail any?"

"Maybe," he looked at her face, "I mean, yes."

"What about your family?"

"We aren't that close."

"You aren't going to invite your parents to your own wedding?"

"Well, my mom passed away, and I didn't want to bother my dad."

"I'm sorry about your mother, what happened?"

"Cancer."

"So, did you fall out with your dad before or after she passed?" she asked.

"Fall out? I never fell out with my dad?"

"Then why wouldn't invite him to your wedding?"

"We just aren't . . . you know . . . close," Byron stuttered out.

"I guess, it's none of my business, but I think you should invite your dad. If your only son doesn't invite you to his wedding, you might take it personally."

Julie was spot on, as usual, and he knew it. "You are right, I'll send him an invite."

"You might want to start with a phone call, before you send the invitation in the mail."

"Yeah, good point."

However, two days later as he walked out of the second tux rental shop that had nothing for the weekend he needed it, he still hadn't gotten around to calling his dad. That's when he got a text from Julie. "How'd your call go with your dad?"

Rather than respond that it hadn't gone at all, he decided to get it over with. So, for the first time since his mother died and not on his dad's birthday, he called home.

"Hello."

"Hi, Dad. It's Byron."

"Hey son, um, you okay?"

"Yeah, I am just calling to say I'm getting married."

"Wow … not that it's surprising, but, wow. Great. Congratulations."

"I was calling to see if you wanted to come."

"You bet, when is it?"

"A week from Friday."

The pause made it clear that it was sooner than his dad expected. So, Byron continued, "If you can't make it, I totally understand."

"No, no, I'll be there. I wouldn't miss it."

"Great, an invitation will be there in a few days with all the details."

"I'll watch for it."

There was their common pause and Byron was about to go to the standard, "I better get going," when Dad asked, "Do you need anything? I mean I could help pay for something. I know weddings can be expensive."

"No, Dad, that's fine. We have it all covered."

"Can't I do something to help?"

"Not unless you have a tuxedo to rent. I guess we chose a popular weekend to get hitched."

"I've got my tux, from my wedding."

"Oh Dad, that's fine, you don't have to bring it. I'm sure I can figure something out."

"It wouldn't be any trouble. After all, it might as well go to use. It's just been sitting in the closet. It should fit as . . . " His dad tried to determine how to ask this delicately, but nothing came to mind. "I mean, as long as you haven't gained too much weight."

"I still wear the same size I did in college." While this was true, it was only because, as a doctor, he had been in college for a long time. And while the same size did fit, it took considerably more pulling and squeezing to get into than it used to.

"Great, then I'll bring it."

And he did. Once inside, Dad placed his suitcase on the ground and pulled out a long, black suit bag on top.

"Here you go, son."

"Thanks for bringing it." Byron quickly showed his father to his room. "Well, the ceremony is tomorrow at 9:30 a.m. so, we better leave around 9:00. I don't want to be late for my own wedding."

"Sounds good. Good night, son."

"Good night, Dad."

Byron turned toward his room.

"Oh, and son."

"Yes," Byron responded as he turned back to his dad. It took a second for his dad to get it out, but he eventually said, "Congratulations, I'm very proud of you."

Byron paused. He wasn't used to his dad showing any emotion and he could tell that the last line was as hard for his father to deliver as it was for him to hear. "Yeah . . . thanks, Dad. Good night. And let me know if you need anything."

"Will do, good night."

Byron dashed off to his room, anxious to end the awkwardness and to see if the tuxedo would indeed fit. He had wanted to wear his regular suit, but Julie was adamant that if it wasn't a tuxedo, it wouldn't look like a real wedding, and Byron had no intention of disappointing her at this point. Over the last few weeks, he had become well acquainted with her and it wasn't that he feared her, but she did have a presence that portrayed certain expectations. Truth was, he enjoyed making her happy. And while he would never admit it to anyone, especially himself, he was going to miss spending time with Julie.

Perhaps he would have been able to explore these feelings in more detail if other fears were not rising in his gut as the zipper descended on the suite bag. Whether the tuxedo fit had been his top concern, but no more. He raced through the flashcards of his memory to try to recall if he had ever seen a picture of his parents at their wedding.

While the fast-paced world of fashion, particularly women's fashion, changed all the time, the simple elegant tuxedo had changed very little. Or at least that is what Byron had assumed until that zipper had finished its descent.

He was face to face with proof that a tuxedo from the 1970's and the tuxedo of today had diverged in a major way. Before him was a baby blue jacket and pants. To match a white shirt and in place of the vertical pleats so common down the face of tuxedo shirts of today was curled lace with swirled baby blue threading to tie it back to the rest of the ensemble. And to complete the set, the baby blue bow tie and cummerbund fell to the floor.

Even as brief as his dad was, he thought when he had offered his tuxedo he could have mentioned that no human had been seen wearing such a suite since John Lennon had sung with the Beatles.

Five minutes later he had verified that, while tight, it did indeed fit, but could he wear it? Julie had said she wanted a tuxedo, but while she may be upset if he showed up in a boring black suit, she might shoot him if he showed up in this baby blue beauty that reflected back at him in the mirror. If only they were getting wed at the end of a Halloween ball.

His dad expected him to wear the tuxedo. Julie expected him to wear the tuxedo. But if you were trying to avoid your wedding looking like a joke, this may be the wrong attire. He was unsure of what to do, but he was sure of one thing, tomorrow was going to be interesting.

Chapter 9

Asking for Her Hand

Julie woke up the next morning feeling more excited than she expected. Today was the day she shed the oppressive bondage of singlehood forever. She hadn't even fully removed the covers when she heard a slight knock at the door, "Honey, you in there?" Clearly she wasn't the only one excited.

The night before, her parents had flown in from back east, and, at the airport, as her mother caught a glimpse of her, she rushed into her arms totally ignoring any whistles or yellow coats telling them to move on. The only way Julie could think to describe her mother's mood was pure giddiness.

Even now, the gentle tapping on the bedroom door was like that of a child anxious for their parents to get up on Christmas, but cautious of upsetting them. And, just like a child on Christmas morning, Julie's mother had found it difficult to sleep. Today was a day she had dreamed of for a long time.

It was 6 a.m., as late as the enthusiasm would allow her to wait. Again came a gentle knock. "Yes, Mom, I'm here," Julie said as her mother rushed in.

"You haven't even started getting ready yet?"

"Mom, it's 6:00 in the morning, we don't need to be there until 9:30."

"I think we'd better get started."

Julie knew her mom was glad she hadn't started getting ready yet. For years her mom had dreamed of standing in front of a mirror, doing her makeup and putting her hair in an "updo" in preparation for her father to walk her down the aisle. Mom had told her a hundred times and Julie knew she didn't want to miss a second of it.

"I need to shower first."

"Good idea. You shower, and I'll get the makeup and hair items set up and ready to make you look amazing."

Julie had a very nice, very long master bath. It was one of the main reasons she had bought the home. Not only did it have a bath, shower, and a jacuzzi tub, but it also had a large sink, vanity, and mirror she could sit at to do her makeup.

When she bought the home, she pictured herself every morning leisurely applying her eyeshadow and sitting for long jacuzzi tub soaks on the weekend. Now, six years later, the jacuzzi tub sat hardly used. It had long ago turned into a place for her to layout outfits and store clean clothes she hadn't gotten around to putting away. And more makeup was applied in the front seat of her car at stop lights than in front of the vanity, but it was going to be used properly today. Mom was sure of that. So, while Julie showered, Mom arranged and chatted nonstop.

After mostly small talk around what types of braids and twist her hair would be forced into or what tone of base she preferred, Julie decided she could ask what was really on her mind, "Mom, is Dad okay with this?"

"What do you mean? Of course, he is. He couldn't be happier."

"He seemed a little odd last night."

"I wouldn't worry about your father. He is a bit old fashioned, that's all."

"I know he's old fashioned, Mr. Rogers wears more modern sweaters. But what does that have to do with my wedding? I mean, I'm marrying a man, in a church, and we're not even living together. What's more old-fashioned than that?"

"We are very happy about that. He just thinks that meeting Byron before the morning of the wedding would've been nice. But don't worry, he'll be fine."

Julie admitted this was a reasonable request. After all, meeting the parents was a standard rite of passage in any courtship. Had this wedding been happening ten years ago, Julie's mom would also have demanded the opportunity to meet her fiancé, but with Julie into her 30's, she was so happy to see her getting married at all, she wasn't going to get hung up on little details like who he was.

"I told Dad, Byron was picking up his dad at the airport, so he couldn't be there last night."

"Yes, he understood, but he thought it was odd."

"What, that he had to pick up his dad?"

"No, the whole situation."

"What do you mean?"

"Julie, don't worry about it. You want this day to be perfect. Don't let your father's skepticism bother you. I told him to drop it, so he'll behave today."

"Mom, what do you mean by his skepticism?"

"Forget I said anything."

"Mom, it's my wedding day, I deserve to know what Dad thinks."

"Well . . . "

"Come on, Mom."

She had always been a pushover for her daughter. "I'm not sure your father trusts Byron, or at least, he's a little uncomfortable with him."

"What's he worried about? That he is secretly an axe murderer?"

"That did come up."

"You're kidding, right."

"You are his little girl. Nothing will ever change that. He feels an obligation to ensure that you are safe and don't get hurt."

"Byron's not going to hurt me."

"I know, but your dad doesn't know that. He feels things are a bit rushed. Last night he was rattling on and on about how when he married me, he had to ask my father for permission before he proposed, and then he mentioned something about handbaskets and hell."

"He wanted Byron to ask him before he proposed?"

"He just wanted to be involved with the decision to some small degree. You mean the world to him, but he'll see that Byron's an amazing man. He simply needs time to get to know him. Maybe after he meets him today this will all blow over."

Julie was torn. On one hand, she knew her father's desire to protect her was based in love. But didn't he trust her not to pick an axe murderer? After all, her mother trusted her. But then again, her mother was so anxious for her to get married, if she had found out Byron was an axe murderer, she would likely have said, "Sure everyone seems evil if you only focus on their bad qualities."

"I know what to do."

Her mom suddenly look uneasy as her eyes surveyed Julie's face. "Julie, this will work out. Don't do anything abrupt. Just let it be. There is no reason to call off or postpone the wedding because of your dad."

"I have no plans on postponing my wedding. Mom, go and tell dad to get ready quickly. We are going to the church at 8:30. I have a phone call to make."

She wasn't comfortable with the idea, but her mother obeyed. After all, it was Julie's wedding day. Once she left the room and the door was shut, Julie picked up her phone.

Saturdays were Byron's only day to sleep in, and even though today was his wedding day, he did not plan to make an exception. Yet the sound that was pulling him into and out of his dreams was not his typical alarm. By the time his brain focused enough to realize it was an incoming call, it had already gone to voicemail.

Grateful for voicemails, he rolled back over hoping he could find his way back into his dream. While he wasn't completely sure what the dream was, he had been flying, getting some award, or perhaps eating cheesecake, whatever it was, it was good. But just as hope of reentering slumber was becoming a reality, the phone rang again. Byron willed his eyes to focus onto the faceplate of the phone. "Julie?" Instantly the thought that she was backing out flashed through his mind. After all, who doesn't have cold feet on their wedding day? Byron would have further contemplated the correlation between our likelihood of taking action to the temperature of one's extremities but decided he better answer the phone. After all, no matter how bad the news, sending Julie to voicemail a second time wasn't going to make it better.

"Hello?"

"Did I wake you up?" Julie said.

He knew a lie would be futile but contemplated it long enough for Julie to jump in. "Nevermind, it doesn't matter. I need you to be at the church by 8:30."

"8:30? Why? It's a little late for a run through."

"Not for that, I want you to meet my mom and dad." Byron felt the temperature of his feet dropping. "And ask my father for my hand," Julie added.

"What?"

"I said, and ask my father for my hand."

"No, I heard you, but, do people . . . even do that anymore?"

"You do."

"Isn't it a little late in the game?"

"This is not a game," Julie said.

"I didn't mean that, but I'm not sure I'm comfortable asking your dad, whom I've never met, for your hand in marriage an hour before we are supposed to be married."

There was a moment of silence, where again Byron wished he had been a little more awake because then perhaps he would have practiced the "think first, speak second" theory he spent so much time preaching to his clients.

"Byron, this is important to me, can you be at the church at 8:30, and ask my father for my hand?"

"What if he says no?"

"Oh, I forgot to add, and do whatever you have to in order to get his consent?"

Byron at this point debated asking, "Or else you'll what?" But he had been awake a little longer now and thought, worst case, she backs out. Or was there something worse? He decided he didn't want to find out, and her backing out was not a good outcome either. So, he simply said, "See you at 8:30."

Byron took a deep breath and headed for the shower.

Solomon said, "It shall be well with them that fear God." And the wise king was not alone in the subject. Indeed, it seemed to be a prerequisite to get your stuff published in the Old Testament that you love the word "begat" and that you have a good working knowledge of this God-fearing thing. Byron had never felt he had a good grasp on the topic, but as he approached the towering, solid, decorative, 10-foot front doors of the St. Mark's Lutheran Church, he felt his grasp of the concept improving.

Fear was exactly what he felt as the door slowly began to swing under Byron's pull. It was a fear he never felt for the mild-mannered man, the father he only ever called Dad, who walked up the steps behind him. In fact, he could only think of two times he'd ever felt true intense fear of meeting someone. One was now, and the other was the first time he came up these stairs. Both times he was on his way to meet a man behind this door, and both went by father.

He had not crossed the threshold before he heard Julie, in an angry whisper, "Byron, what are you wearing?"

The attire of his forefathers had the impact he assumed it would have.

"Julie," he began as he finished his entrance and allowed his father to enter, "This is Stanley, my dad. He was kind enough to bring me his tux from his wedding for me to wear," he said.

"Oh, so you are Julie," Byron's father said, then added with a resonance of sincerity, "You look beautiful. I'm so happy for you and Byron and so glad I get to be here."

"Thank you, I'm glad to meet you as well." Julie greeted her soon-to-be father-in-law with a warm smile. She then turned to Byron and her face lost any sign of warmth. And he knew exactly why. Clearly, she had instantly forgiven her father for the baby blue disaster he now wore but he could see he would not be so easily forgiven. She made that clear as she pulled him aside and resumed her angry whisper that comes so naturally to all mothers, wives, and, as Julie proved, soon-to-be wives, when under the roof of any sacred edifice. "What are you wearing?"

"It is, *technically*, a tux," Byron whispered back.

"Yes, it is *technically* a tux. But the fact that you have to add the word technically in front of it should have been a clue to wear something else. What is my father going to say when he sees you in that get up?"

Byron shrugged, partially because he could sense the question was rhetorical and partially because he had no idea.

"Well, I'm sure it won't impress Dad. He's waiting in Father Young's office. She pointed to a small room that sat at the back of the church where they had originally met with Father Young. It was only now that Byron noted Father Young sitting on a pew a few rows from the back, not knowing what to do with himself since Julie had commandeered his office.

"Remember," Julie continued, "you need to get his permission to marry me." She forced a smile and added, "Good luck."

Byron wanted to remind her that there was no game plan if her father said no, but decided there was no point, took a deep breath and opened the door.

An older man dressed in a suite matching the one Byron now wished he had been in sat at the desk. Byron instantly saw Julie's face in his. He was definitely her dad. He stood as Byron entered, "Hello, you must be Byron."

"Yes, and you must be . . . " Byron let this hang in the air. When he had begun this sentence, his intentions were entirely pure. However, it was about the third word in when he realized Julie always called him Dad, and Byron couldn't recall ever learning his name. It must have been on the invitation, so he concentrated hard on trying to envision what it had said but was coming up blank. Percy came to mind, or some weird "P" name, but should he risk guessing? The pause had been long enough that Dad jumped in.

"Pelham."

"Oh, yeah that's right. Sorry about that. I'm a bit nervous."

"Don't feel bad. It's an odd name. Even the man I'm named after didn't go by it. Most people called him Plum but since I never could pass for a fruit, I've been stuck with Pelham."

"Well, it's good to meet you."

"I'm glad to *finally* be meeting you."

Byron wasn't sure how to do this. He'd never asked a man for his daughter's hand before. He felt like some small talk was in order, something to lighten the mood but nothing came to mind. Byron's discomfort was obvious, his face was flush, sweat was forming on his forehead and many more less visible places. If Pelham shared his discomfort, he didn't show it.

"Well . . . Pilgrim." Pelham let the mistake slide as Byron continued to stammer. "I . . . uh . . . was wondering . . . ?"

"Yes," Pelham said.

"I'm not really sure how to say this, but can I marry your daughter?"

"It looks to me that you are going to, so I suppose you *can*."

Oh great, the old *may* versus *can*. He had sworn in sixth grade he'd never fall for that one again. "What I mean is, do we . . . would we . . . may we," Byron wanted to get the right word. "Have your blessing?"

"Byron, I have known you for a grand total of less than five minutes, we haven't had a phone call, a text, a letter, or even a comment on each other's Facebook page. And now you are asking me if I am okay with trusting the most important thing in the world to me, the protection, happiness, and welfare of my little girl to a total stranger. What would you do?"

Byron had never thought of this from her father's perspective, what if it were his daughter getting involved in a sham wedding. The pressure was mounting and rather than take it, Byron was buckling, a sick feeling in his stomach began to grow. The only answer he could come up with was, "I wouldn't give my consent, and you can't. I understand, Pilgrim, the show must not go on." Byron was trying to build up the courage to say it. But the more he thought, the more sick he got and he began to realize that if he opened his mouth he might throw up.

But it was Pelham, the pillar of strength that first buckled.

"But I realize, there is no point in laying all this on you at this point. There's no turning back now, huh?"

Byron wasn't sure he was grateful that he had been saved from answering. Despite not having to answer the difficult question, the sick feeling still lingered.

Pelham now had a calm kindness in his voice as he asked, "What was the point of pulling me aside to ask when you knew it was too late to matter?"

Byron thought and honestly prevailed, "Because, it was what Julie wanted."

Pelham looked at Byron and tears began to well up. "I guess sitting down with her ornery, old man and asking for my consent wasn't easy, but you did it, because it's what Julie wanted." He chuckled a little as he spoke. "She always gets her way. Always has. I guess you have me to blame for that. I've always been a pushover for Julie. And if she wants you, and she wants my blessing, then I guess you and I better give it to her."

Byron sighed. The sick feeling had not completely dissipated but he was now feeling confident he'd make it without throwing up, when Pelham continued, "But promise me you'll always put her first, care for her, and fight for what she needs?"

The sickness came back stronger than ever. Pelham was staring into Byron's eyes.

"Of course," Byron quickly got out, more out of reflex than anything else.

"Well, then I guess you are now my son, or will be soon enough," Pelham said as he put his arm around Byron and headed for the door. "By the way son, I love the tux. I tried to wear one just like it when I got married, but I guess Barbara isn't as open minded as Julie. My day had a real flair for fashion, especially compared to the boring stuff these days. Glad you see it."

The talk had clearly calmed Pelham but inside Byron there was anything but calm.

Chapter 10

The Ceremony

By the time Byron and Pelham emerged from the little office in the back of the chapel, the wedding was only ten minutes from kick-off. Julie and her mother had both done a marvelous job of looking nothing but happy as they greeted family and guests. But their true feelings were manifest by the frequent, nervous glances towards the door of the little office.

The faces of the two men walking out of the door told two very different stories. Byron, who emerged first, looked like he was preparing to audition for a part in The Walking Dead, and when Julie caught sight of him, she thought for sure the wedding was off—that is, until she saw her dad.

She hadn't seen him look this excited since he had paid for the final semester of her college tuition.

Julie and Barbara both, from opposite sides of the church, abruptly abandoned their conversations with relatives and dashed towards Pelham and Byron. But before they reached them, Father Young cut them off. "We really need for everyone to get into their places," he said.

Julie's face was pleading to know what had happened. Her dad spoke up, "All right, everyone to their places." As he spoke, he grabbed Julie's arm and gave a little push to send Byron in the right direction toward the front of the church.

Pelham, in an effort to continue his orchestration, leaned into his bride of many years, "Don't worry, hun. I've got it covered. You can go and take your seat." Byron had started his movement to the front of the chapel, but his pace was not brisk, nor linear. "Come to think of it, maybe you'd better help Byron," he added.

She walked up and helped steady Byron who had begun to tilt with nausea.

"Daddy, what happened?" Julie asked without allowing the top and bottom of her mouth to separate from one another, as they headed to the back of the chapel.

"You have a good man, Julie. He asked for your hand and I gave my consent."

"Then why does he look like you punched him in the gut?"

"Does he? I thought he looked dapper when I was with him. Nice tux, did you pick that?"

"No!"

"Well, don't worry about it. Maybe he's just a little nervous. After all, it is his wedding day."

It is not at all uncommon for there to be a slow dramatic walk down the aisle during a wedding, but it's less commonly done by the groom and his soon-to-be mother-in-law. Byron was not sure why this nice older lady had taken his arm, but he was grateful for it.

She was saying something but he couldn't make it out. His body was preoccupied with two tasks: keeping the monster growing in his gut at bay and playing over and over again in his mind Pelham's words, "Promise me you will always put her first, care for her, and fight for her needs." Nothing in this was above and beyond what he knew he was about to promise in his vows but, coming from her loving father, it hit in a new way. His whole career was about protecting such vows, was he desecrating all he stood for? Was he betraying her father, her mother, Julie herself? Wasn't he robbing her of any chance of ever having real love. With too much focus on the mind, he almost forgot to keep his stomach from making an entrance and things began to bubble in his throat. He regained his focus on his gut and willed everything back down.

His rather slow saunter down the aisle had come to an end and Byron now stood at the feet of Father Young. Julie's mother, having gotten the package to its destination, went ahead and took her seat. Left to stand on his own, Byron decided he better take a seat as well and did so on the front pew. No sooner had he sat down then he felt a small tap on his shoulder. Turning around, he made out the blurry outline of his secretary, Ms. Whitacker. "I'm so excited to be here. It's really happening! I worried this day would never come. I am so happy and proud of you. It reminds me of when I married Tom. I wish he were here. He loved weddings. We even went to his father's second wedding, after he ran off with his secretary and left his mother. That one was a little awkward. But don't you worry, I won't be letting you run off with me."

Byron loved Ms. Whitacker. She was always fun and helpful around the office but now her rather high-pitch whisper was not helping settle either his stomach or mind. He attempted a small smile but didn't dare attempt speech. Luckily, the organ began to play the wedding march.

Julie and Pelham right on cue, began their own, much less wobbly, walk down the aisle. Julie was radiant. Truly a beautiful bride, one worth all the attention that should have been shown her at this moment, but most eyes were fixed on the front of the chapel where Father Young was trying to beckon Byron to stand up without abandoning his post. Byron's head was down until Ms. Whitacker, always anxious to help, tapped Byron again on the shoulder and pointed kindly to Father Young who continued his beckoning. Byron looked up, saw the beckoning and held up the "one minute" finger.

Julie kept her cadence between walk and organ, but her face showed worry as she noted Byron's lack of uprightness. He noted her concern but couldn't worry about what she needed. As he tried to calm his inner churning, he recalled when Julie had her own battle with shock when she was driving. He tried to employ his own methods and slowly count while he breathed in and out, but he couldn't get his mind off the continuing cadence of the wedding march and the idea that no slowly counted breaths could help.

Byron, continued his deep breathing and forced himself to ignore his brain and put all his energy on his nausea. His goal was simple, have the nausea far enough under control to be able to stand up by the time Julie made it to the front. Not standing for his bride while she walked down the aisle he knew was not kosher but he figured him sitting was preferable to him passing out, and he wasn't Jewish. As Julie came to the front, Byron took a deep breath and stood with a little help from Pelham.

Father Young, happy everyone was standing and in place, quickly began. "Dearly beloved and honored guests, we are gathered together here to join Julie Smith and Byron Lewis in the spiritual union of marriage."

Up to this point Byron thought he might just be on the mend but that all changed as Father Young said, "This contract is not to be entered into lightly but thoughtfully and seriously and with deep realization of its obligations and responsibilities."

Father Young had told Byron and Julie that these would be the words of the vows and at the time he had thought nothing of it. But now his nausea once again grew and grew as Father Young continued, "Please remember love, loyalty, and understanding are the foundations of a happy and enduring home."

"Julie and Byron will now exchange rings as a symbol of their love and commitment."

Byron panicked slightly, had he remembered the ring. But, as was usually the case, his Father was prepared. He handed the ring to Byron who, after a few more breaths to calm his stomach, took it out and placed it on Julie's finger. As Julie leaned in close to place the ring on Byron's finger she whispered, "You okay?" Byron nodded as he closed his eyes and continued his deep breathing.

"Do you, Julie Smith, take this man, Byron Lewis, to be your lawfully wedded husband, to have and to hold, in sickness," Byron was sure this was particularly apt right now, "and in health, in good times and woe, for richer and poorer, keeping yourself unto him for as long as you both shall live?"

"I do."

Julie's confident and straightforward answer impressed Byron and gave him some strength. It also made him wonder how she could be so calm at a time like this.

He needed to prepare himself. It was his turn and, as much as he wished he had Julie's confidence, he knew it would be all he could muster to simply say anything.

"Do you, Byron Lewis, take this woman, Julie Smith, to be your lawfully wedded wife." Sometimes knowing what is coming makes us more prepared and better able to handle what we must face, but sometimes the knowledge only seems to exacerbate the feelings, good or bad, that we feel. His stomach went from churning to high-speed mixer as he knew Father Young's words before he said them, "To have and to hold, in sickness and in health, in good times and in woe." That was it.

He was promising to have and to hold someone he never planned to see again, what was he to do? Yell out, "I can't do it"? Admit in front of everyone it was a sham? Julie would kill him. No alternative seemed fair to her. On the one hand if he said, "I do," he would be robbing her of her chance at real love and true companionship, not to mention making a mockery of the vows he worked so hard in others to preserve. On the other hand, if he didn't, he would have led her along, made her show up for her own wedding day only to embarrass her in front of all her family and friends. He didn't know what to do, and his indecision only made him feel all the more nauseated. But despite his swirling thoughts and mixing insides, Father Young marched on.

"For richer, or poorer, keeping yourself unto her as long as you both shall live?"

Every eye was on Byron. He took two deep breaths and said, "I . . ." Vomit began to rise. He paused, forced it down, lightly belched, held his hand over his mouth in embarrassment, and, as a safety precaution, took two more breaths and quickly said, "do."

There was an audible sucking of air as everyone in the building drew in breath.

It was done, but that did nothing to help Byron feel any better, and he wondered if he'd done the right thing as the room began to spin.

"By the authority vested in me, I now pronounce you husband and wi—" Halfway through the last word, Byron could hold it no more and vomit projected from deep within his troubled gut straight onto the front of Father Young. Byron's stomach finally felt better, but the rest of his body had had enough. Everything went black.

Chapter 11

The Wedding Night

Byron woke up to see a bright light shining ahead of him. He would have assumed he was dead except for the paramedic standing behind it.

"Oh good, you're not dead. I thought I was going to be the world's fastest widow," came the voice of Julie standing behind the paramedic.

"I don't know, I've seen some pretty fast widows," said Byron with a weak smile.

"Glad to see that the trauma of our wedding didn't damage your corny sense of humor."

The paramedic helped him sit up and gave him a drink. "You feel okay?" he asked.

"I think I'll be okay. I'm feeling much better now."

"I think he'll be fine," the parametric said to Julie. "Give him plenty of fluids and no strenuous activity for the next day or two."

The paramedic picked up his bag and then left. Julie was now alone with Byron in Father Young's office.

"So, what happened out there?" Julie asked.

"I felt really sick."

"I figured out that much."

"I guess I was more nervous than I expected."

"Is marrying me, even though you won't have to see me, really that scary?"

"It wasn't you. It just sort of hit me." He wanted to tell her more. Share about how the idea of their marriage kind of tore him apart. And that as he went to actually go forward with it, he felt this was a serious commitment that he wasn't taking seriously. But the trust needed for that conversation was not there yet, even if they were husband and wife. After all, she didn't have any issue. Saying he wasn't taking it seriously enough would only be insinuating that she wasn't either. He had no desire to implicate her.

"I wonder what everyone thought?"

"I'll tell you what they thought. My Aunt Maybell said, 'He must sure know how to throw a good bachelor party.'"

"Oh great, they think I'm a drunk."

"Don't worry about them. Most of them are my family, and we have our share of drunks. Not only that, you can take comfort in the fact that you'll never have to see them again. I'm just glad you're feeling better." This was said with more sincerity than Byron expected for someone's who's wedding day he had just ruined. Perhaps she really did care about him.

And speaking of their wedding day, Byron had to ask, "Are we married?"

"I think they are going to let us slip under the bar. Or at least I got this." Julie held up their wedding certificate. "Father Young said the only part we didn't get to before you baptized him in stomach acid was the kiss. Which, no offense, I wasn't looking forward to. Given the circumstances, I mean. "

Byron wasn't sure if she meant the fact that they didn't love each other or that he had just vomited, so despite being a bit wounded, he said, "I understand."

"Someone noted I might get a chance to give you mouth to mouth instead but I had seen what just came out of you, and I also noticed you were still breathing."

Byron wasn't sure he liked the order she noted those two items and almost asked what she would have done if he hadn't been breathing, but decided he better not ask questions he didn't want the answer to.

"Where is everyone else?"

Most people went home, only ones left are your secretary, my friend Becky, and our parents."

"So, what's the plan from here?" Byron asked.

"What do you mean?"

"What's next?"

A startled, almost frightened look flashed across her face. "What do you mean? You go your way, and I go mine."

"Yeah," Byron was now confused. "But how? We can't go out in the parking lot and walk into our separate cars and wave goodbye to our parents and each other at the same time. Might not go over too well."

With the realization that he meant short term and not long term, Julie sighed. "I have that all planned. I thought we talked about it."

"If you did, it left my mind as completely as my breakfast left my stomach."

"Well, we walk out and convince everyone you're okay. That part is new. My mom will cry, we hug and then walk. We ignore Father Young scrubbing the carpet at the front of the church, probably also crying. Head out the front steps, they toss rice as we walk down to your car, which no doubt is covered in Oreos, streamers, silly string, and a just married sign in the back window."

"My car?"

"Don't interrupt. It will wash off. Then you will drive me across town to the Hampton Inn, that I have a reservation at. See, my parents will be at my home for one more night. They are driving my car home. You drive off. Is your dad staying in town tonight?"

"No, he flies out this afternoon."

"Okay, then you drive around, do some shopping or whatever you want until your dad leaves and you go home. I get a great night's sleep, take an Uber home in the morning, we both get the link with the photos from the photographer, print a few and then go back to our separate lives."

And so it was. Well, mostly. Julie forgot to mention a few points. First, after everyone was assured Byron was truly okay, sensing this may be the last time he would see Byron for a while, his father held him close, and then pulled him away and, while still bracing his shoulders, looked at him. It was a look Byron had never really seen in his father. It was contentment and pride, honor, love, and esteem. It was a look every boy instinctively hopes to see in the eyes of their father. It expressed fulfillment of expectations for both father and son. More clearly, then the limitations of words could express. It said, "Son, you are now a man."

Byron didn't know this existed and yet knew he had always wanted it. And while a rush of joy began to flow, it was quickly tempered with inadequacy. For he knew what led his father to look at him like that was all falsehoods. The moment was beautiful, but it was built on lies. And poor foundations don't discriminate based on the beauty of the edifice, and Byron knew it.

The next departure between Julie's carefully crafted future and reality was the next father. Pelham embraced Byron as he went through the line and whispered in his ear. "She's yours now, remember your promise and you'll do fine." Instantly, the nausea had found its way back home. But with nothing left in his stomach to churn and expel, it didn't last.

From that point, Julie's version got back on track, the crying mother, the rice, the decorated car and ultimately Byron found himself parked below the archway marking the entrance to the Hampton Inn across town.

Throwing the car into park, he said, "I'll get the door," as he hopped out and began to help Julie out of the passenger seat. Her outfit was much more traditional than his and the poof of her wedding dress didn't make the exit from the vehicle easy. Once standing upright, she retrieved her bag from the back seat and the two stood awkwardly for a minute.

"Well, I guess this is . . . " Byron paused, "Goodbye." He couldn't think of a better word but hated it once it came out. They both did. It seemed too cold, too final, and, while they didn't like it, neither could contradict it.

"I'll send you your first check to the routing number you gave me, first of the month," Byron continued.

"You know, I feel kind of bad about taking the money," Julie responded. "After all, this will benefit me too."

"No, a deal is a deal, and I always stand by my word."

Another long pause. The eyes traveled from the ground to each other and then back to the ground.

"Well, I guess I better go," Julie reluctantly said.

"Um . . . oh . . . .well . . . okay."

They looked at each other and both leaned in for a hug. It was more than a goodbye. It expressed friendship, an honest gladness for having known one another, and, most importantly, desire. Not a desire for passion, but a desire for this to be more, more than goodbye, more than a short-lived friendship that ended in a long-distance marriage of convenience, and in the emotion of the hug, Julie turned her head and gave Byron a small peck on the cheek.

Shocked, Byron instantly let go, and just as instantly said, "Thank you."

"Thank you?" Julie asked, "For what?"

The honest answer was "the kiss" but Byron's instincts had stopped and while Julie would have loved the honest answer, and may have replied with, "If you liked that, try this on for size." But he would never know, because Byron, in an effort to cover his instinctive reply, to what he now saw as a kindly gesture, no more than one would give to an aunt when saying hello in many cultures, said, "For being willing to marry me and go on this journey. Not everyone would be willing to marry someone they would never see again."

The reminder of the words "never see" was sufficient to end whatever moment they had.

"Well, thank you. I think it will work well for us both. Have a good one." And with that, Julie headed toward the doors that slid open and then shut behind her. Byron shortly thereafter pulled out, leaving his bride to approach a front desk clerk who, given his view of their last exchange, had a very confused look on his face.

As Julie had predicted, Byron did a little shopping to ensure there was no chance encounter with his father, grabbed a bite to eat, and then headed home. Early evening found him sitting, wondering what he did with his nights before they had been filled with nightly calls to Julie to go over wedding plans. It was only six weeks ago and yet it felt like an earlier, distant life. And as much as the past without her seemed distant, a future without her seemed impossible. He wasn't in love, or at least that is what he kept saying to himself. He simply liked her company. And he began to think of an excuse to call, as he stared down at her contact information on his cell phone.

Julie wasn't enjoying the relaxing evening at the hotel she had envisioned either. Six weeks ago, when things were on her mind, she'd always call Becky, but she had worked hard to avoid her over the past six weeks. She didn't want all the piercing questions about Byron, and how they met, and how could it be happening so fast and what if she had asked, "That isn't the guy from the newspaper?" So, she had limited her contact with Becky. Wedding plans with Byron had more than filled the void, but with no more plans, the void was very apparent. And she couldn't exactly restart calling Becky tonight. "I'm just sitting around on the first night of my honeymoon, thought I'd give you a call." Probably wasn't the right way to restart their relationship, especially if she hoped to avoid questions about her marriage. The other option was Byron. She really didn't have a reason to call but she always enjoyed talking to him. Maybe, she should just call.

So, both sat looking at each other's contact information on their cell phones. But Byron and Julie had agreed that after marriage, no contact, and unfortunately for both, they had married someone who was true to their words. So, while phones were stared at a plenty, neither rang.

Chapter 12

The Honeymoon

Julie arrived at work early the following Monday. She wanted to make sure everything was ready. A refreshing Sunday had helped her get over her sorrow of not having Byron to talk to and she was ready to begin her new life as a married, albeit distantly, woman.

The week previous, she had taken leave. This not only gave her time to finalize all the wedding plans, but also gave her sufficient time off for people to assume she had been on a honeymoon. They didn't need to know she had just been married the past Saturday.

She was well prepared; she even acquired a new name plate. Julie had debated legally changing her name, but it was too much effort, so instead the name plate that once read Julie Smith now simply read, "Mrs. Julie Smith." No one really put the prefix on their name plate but she would break the mold if it proved to the world, particularly Larry's world, that she was indeed married.

She had also printed out several pictures of her and Byron. She was now trying various places in the office to place them. Once they all had a home, she pulled out a thumb drive with an updated slide-show to use as a screensaver. Throughout the last few weeks, she had taken selfies of herself and Byron at almost every place they had gone. And she had quite a convincing collection to play across her screen. Sitting back, she looked over her handy work with satisfaction. No one visiting this office would dare say that this was the office of an old maid. Instead, it was clearly a happily married, not to hit on, set up with, or feel pity for, woman.

Her work was just like any other day. But all her little efforts were paying off. At a morning meeting, Jan noticed her ring and congratulations followed. When Ryan came in to hand her a set of plans, he noticed the picture and asked, "Who's this?"

"That's my husband, Byron," came her ready reply.

"You're married?"

"Yup, just recently."

He too followed with congratulations.

And when the boss walked by, he asked, "How was your time off?"

"It was great."

"Are these pictures new . . . wait . . . did you get married?"

"Yes, I did."

Then he said the thing all the co-workers had said in their head but were not willing to say out loud. "Oh, I guess you really did have a boyfriend."

"You thought I made him up?" Julie said.

Her boss instantly regretted allowing his tongue to outpace his better judgment and defensively said, "No, of course not. Although, Larry was convinced you did."

"You can't trust anything Larry says." Boy, that felt good to say.

"Well, you have a good day," the boss said on his way out.

Julie muttered as he left, "Oh trust me, I will."

But as good as all this felt, the real moment of glory wouldn't be until Larry walked through her door. And this was the one point that had been the grey lining on an otherwise perfect day. By this point in the day Larry had usually interrupted her at least four times. It would be just like him to call in sick on the only day of his existence that Julie was actually looking forward to seeing him.

For a brief moment, Julie contemplated walking by his cube, simply to verify he was in. But, where was his cube? She had avoided seeing him for so long that she had forgotten exactly where he sat. Not that she never needed to get a hold of him. After all, he was the drafting lead on several of her projects, but if she ever had something to show him or give him, she put it on the side of her desk, knowing that in a few minutes he'd be poking his head in. Now that she thought about it, it wasn't just things for Larry. She often set items for other people aside, thinking, "I'll have Larry grab it when he comes by and take it to them."

She felt a brief moment of panic as she thought all this effort might put an end to her free office delivery service. But the benefits were great and that wasn't even counting the added exercise, and this put her mind at ease. And right on cue, Larry's little pointy head made its entrance, "Hey JuJu bug, miss me. I was off this morning getting my pearly whites cleaned. I want to keep your view top notch." The smile he gave was almost as obnoxious as he was.

"It's Julie, or better yet, you can call me Mrs. Smith."

"Mrs? I hate to break it to you, babe, but that's usually not given as an honorary title."

"Very funny, Larry."

"Thanks. I am pretty clever."

"For your information, I am very, very happy to let you know that while I was out, I got married."

"Yeah right . . . nice try. To who? Your imaginary . . . " His face looked much like Prince Humperdinck when he discovered Wesley, very much alive and in the bedroom of his fiancé.

"Oh, you like that picture. It was taken of Byron and me," she paused, "on our wedding day." She had purposely chosen the photo that was displayed most predominantly because the perspective made Byron look rather tall and impressive.

"Lovely," he said as clearly as anyone whose world had just crashed down around his perfectly clean teeth could. "You know . . . I was . . . well . . . just kidding this whole time. I knew he was real. If you'll excuse me, I need to run to a meeting." Julie smiled as he walked out knowing he wouldn't be returning anytime soon.

Julie wasn't the only one who was finding wedded bliss. Monday mornings were not Byron's favorite, but today had a special feeling in the air. Today, he was going to work not only as a marriage counselor but a married marriage counselor. He would never have to hear his clients say, "Well, how would you know?," "You wouldn't understand," or, his favorite, "That's easy for a single guy to say." The gold band still gleaned from its newness. It was probably thicker than most bands, but he wanted the fact that he was married to be noticed rather than spoken. As long as nothing was said, he wouldn't have to mention the fact that he was a newlywed, at least not to his new clients.

He had been around long enough to realize that no one took newlyweds seriously. Whenever his clients commented on seeing a couple that looked like they were enjoying being together, they would quickly say, "Oh, they must be newlyweds, like they know anything about marriage." He continued to think of ways of helping his clients realize he was married without getting himself labeled as in the "honeymoon stage."

Byron's first act was to give birth to a small army of fake internet profiles that were now running a rather successful "Dr. Lewis is a happily married man" PR campaign. For every comment on RateMyCouncilor.com or similar site that scathed about his lack of a ring, certificate, and therefore qualification, was met with a response from harleys4life343 or balletmom751647 (It appears ballet is really making a comeback) saying, "Not that it matters, because councilors can be good, even if not married, but you might want to check your facts, because I know for a fact, Dr. Lewis is happily married."

Byron had been torn if the "happily" was too much. He had deleted it, put it back, and then deleted it about five times before ultimately saying, "I am married, and I'm happy, so I'm happily married."

As weeks rolled on, it became clear that balletmom751647 knew how to run a PR campaign. The number of dropped clients was doing just that, dropping, while the number of new clients was expanding.

Byron was even allowing himself to do the one thing he swore he would never do, use his own experience in his counseling. "You know, Mr. Jordan, I find in my relationship, sometimes my wife needs her space, some time alone, some 'me' time. Maybe you just need to give her some room."

Often in defense of marriage, and his billable rate, Byron would say to clients, "Marriage is one of the best life and financial decisions you will ever make." And, for him, it was true. The improved business far more than made up what he had to pay Julie each month. He couldn't see a downside to this marriage thing. That is, until his secretary fell in love.

Chapter 13

Mounting Excuses

Many men, when faced with the alternative of a wife at home who finds it hard to muster the same passion and emotion she once did as she rounds forty, chases kids, and deals with the realities of middle age and the secretary at work who is paid full time to meet his every request, finds himself more and more in love with his secretary.

Byron was no different, and the love he had for his assistant, Ms. Whitaker, had been growing for a long time. And the feelings were very much mutual.

Ms. Whitaker had been with Byron since the first day he launched his own practice. Their love was as strong and perhaps stronger than most mothers have for their sons. She was like a mother to him, a rebellious, nonconforming, but loving, mother. She had been there when his mother died, and even attended the funeral.

Likewise, when Mrs. Whitaker had become Ms. Whitaker due to the untimely death of her husband, Byron became her closest confidant.

So, it was not surprising when she came into the office gushing over, wanting to talk. "Byron, you'll never guess what I did this weekend."

"You are absolutely correct. I'll never guess."

"I was in San Diego to watch a Padres game."

"You drove five hours to watch a baseball game? I didn't think you liked baseball."

"I don't. I hate it," Ms. Whitacker said matter-of-factly. "It wasn't the game that was wonderful. See, do you remember the Morgans?"

"Oh, no. What happened?" Byron was always very careful about keeping relationships between doctor and patient very professional. Ms. Whitacker was also careful to keep relationships, she just wasn't so worried about the professional part.

"Why are you so negative? Nothing bad happened."

"Ms. Whitacker, I love that you are the nicest person in the world to everyone who comes through that door. Sometimes, I think some keep coming back to see you, not me. But you really shouldn't hang out with clients. It's not proper."

"Oh, please. I'm not their doctor. Anyways, you can scold me about that later. That's not the point. The point is the Morgans are huge Padres fans."

"So, you're willing to drive five hours to attend an event you hate just to disobey my advice about hanging out with clients?"

"Stop interrupting. Well, they had two sets of tickets and with the extra tickets they decided to invite myself and Daryl Goodman, their widower neighbor. And," she paused for dramatic effect, "he's awww-wesommmme." She even added jazz hands for emphasis.

"Wow, you really like this guy. So, what makes him so awwwwe-sommmmmme?" Byron's imitation was not nearly as energetic.

"Well, for one thing, he hates baseball."

"So, you spent five hours driving to a baseball game, four hours watching a baseball game, and five hours driving back from a baseball game and spent the time bonding with a guy over how much you both hate baseball."

"Yeah. Isn't it great?"

"Well, I am very excited for you."

"I have another date with him on Thursday. Maybe our date after that we could do a double with you and Julie."

"Aren't you getting a little ahead of yourself. You better have date number two before planning number three."

"You're probably right. But I think he is really a good man. I'd love for you to meet him."

"Yeah, we could go to a rock concert and bond over how much we all hate rock concerts."

"What do you and Julie like to do for dates? I know you're a big proponent of dates in marriage."

"Oh, you know the usual stuff."

"What's the usual stuff? The Morgans said you told them that original dates are important." Byron knew this idea of Ms. Whitaker hanging out with clients was a problem.

"We like the usual, but original, usual stuff."

"Oh, original, usual stuff. And what would that be?"

"Well, like eating out is something we like but a little while back we decided to eat at the Eiffel tower downtown because it's an unusual spot."

"I get it. Well, if there is a date number three. I'll have to think of a fun, usual, and original date that you and Julie can come along with."

"That sounds fun, um . . . but Julie was thinking she might go visit her parents for a while."

"Well then maybe date number four."

"She did say she was going to stay for a few weeks."

"A few weeks?"

"Her mom is going through some things, so it might take longer than I'd like." That should buy him some time.

"Well, okay date number five or six. But we will get it worked out. If it gets that far."

Unfortunately for Byron, it did get that far. He could only extend Julie's pretend visit to her parents for so long. So pretty soon, he invented clubs, yoga, charity events, and bird watching trips.

Even persistent Ms. Whitaker eventually gave up on the idea of a double date. And Byron was able to slow down on his made-up wife excuses, which was refreshing. Byron hated lying but like most people, did it when the discomfort of doing it was less than the discomfort caused by facing the truth.

Things moved fairly uneventfully for six months, until snow fell over the Las Vegas valley. A good snowfall happened every ten years or so and for Byron that was far too often. As he walked into the office, it was clear Ms. Whitaker did not share his disdain for snow. She was positively beaming, beyond even her usual brightness.

About halfway through the day when he was between clients, Ms. Whitaker came in and asked, "Did you notice anything different about me today?"

Byron, like most men, hated this game. If he said, "Your hair's different," and it's not, it becomes proof that you don't notice her hair, which for some reason is important. Even the "I'm not sure" answer is admitting failure to observe, which is so easily considered as failure to care. But despite hating the game, he did his best.

"You do seem extra excited. I assumed it was all this horrid white stuff."

"I do love the snow, but there may be another reason for my excitement," and she held out her hand.

She had continued to wear her wedding ring following the death of her husband. It was a modest ring reflective of her and her husband's finances at the time. It was now dwarfed by a ring with a diamond that would have made Mr. T jealous.

"Daryl proposed. We're getting married in June."

"Wow. Congratulations!"

"I can hardly wait. I only wish it could be sooner. But so much to plan and get ready. And even though we haven't worked out the exact date, I still want you and Julie to meet him."

"Yeah, hopefully that will work out."

This was much like parents saying, "we'll see" when their son asked if they are going to get a pet giraffe for Christmas.

"Byron." Her tone implied how much what she was about to say meant to her. "Promise me you'll at least both make it to the wedding."

As much as he wanted to, he couldn't bring himself to disappoint her, not right now.

"I will be there."

"You and Julie both right? I want you both to be at the wedding."

"You bet. Let me know the day and I'll make sure we can make it."

"Thanks, Byron. It means a lot to me."

As Ms. Whitaker went back to her desk in the lobby, Byron began to sweat. Could he really ask Julie to come? It had been a year and a half since the wedding. They had agreed no contact. What would she say if he called up?

Did he even have her number? He had gotten a new phone a few months back and not all his contacts had transferred. Looking in his phone, he saw her, Julie Smith. She was listed with a phone number. Under company was listed the letter B. He wasn't sure what that was, probably a typo. But should he call her? Well, Ms. Whitaker's wedding was 6 months away. No reason to bother Julie now. He should at least wait until they had a date, and who knew, maybe it would get called off. He was a widower. People who were younger than him were dying all the time. He pushed the thought out of his head, but maybe he could come up with a great excuse before then.

Problems plus time rarely led to success but that is exactly what he hoped for now.

"Julie, we are really looking forward to coming. I only wish it could be more than a weekend, but your dad has to go to LA for his conference."

"I'm excited too. It's been a long time."

"We haven't seen you since the wedding. I'd like a chance to really sit down and get to know Byron more."

"Oh . . . yeah, about that."

"Is there something wrong, honey? Is something going on between you and Byron?"

"No, not that, Mom."

"I mean, I realize that the first few years in marriage can be tough."

"Mom, stop. Byron and I are doing fine. It's just that he has to be out of town for work that weekend."

"For work? I thought he was a marriage counselor."

"He is, but he travels."

"For what?"

"For like couple . . . cruise therapy."

"You mean he goes on a cruise with a couple and counsels them?"

"Yeah. He does it all the time."

"Well, your dad will be very disappointed."

"Why's dad going to be disappointed?"

"Don't get me wrong. I'd like to see Byron too, but your dad has been asking a lot about him. Yesterday he asked if we should get his number from you so we could at least talk to him. But I thought he might consider that weird."

"Yes, he would. He will be here next time you come."

"But everything is going good between you two, right?"

"Yes, why do you keep asking?"

"I just want to be sure. You two are . . . you know."

"Mom, if you are asking about intimacy. It's none of your business."

"I was just wondering if we might get a big announcement soon."

"Mom. I've told you before. I'm not pregnant," Julie said.

"Are you sure?"

"Yes, Mom. I'm very sure."

"Are you on birth control? Do you not like kids?" her mom asked.

"I'm not on birth control. And I think kids are wonderful."

"Just not for you."

No matter what they talked about, the conversation seemed to find its way back to this. "No. Just not right now."

"Julie, you're over thirty years old, you don't have many right now's left."

"Don't make me feel old," Julie said.

"It's just biology, time's ticking for all of us. For me too. I don't want to over pressure you, but . . . "

Sure, you don't, Julie thought.

"I think grandkids would be really nice."

Julie knew grandkids were important to her mom and probably her dad, even though he never brought it up. But hearing her talk with so much emotion was hard on Julie and she was starting to feel bad for her mother and in her pity told her what she knew she wanted to hear.

"Mom," she allowed her voice to get quiet and her mother's anticipation rose. "We are trying. It's just getting pregnant isn't as easy as we thought."

She could sense her mother's instant and total relief.

"Honey, I totally understand. Why do you think that you didn't come along until we'd been married for three years? We tried, and tried, and tried."

"All right, Mom."

"No, the reason I am telling you is we found out we were trying too hard."

"I'm not sure I want to hear this story."

Her mother ignored her and continued. "We got so worried that we finally went to see a fertility specialist. And he told us that stress can make it harder to get pregnant. We were stressed and trying too hard."

"Okay, Mom. I think we are done here."

"I only brought it up because a month later you were on your way. So."

"We can try that. I promise we will not stress about it but only if we talk about something else right now."

"I'm so happy you're trying. I'll let you know if I come up with any pointers. We can't wait to see you soon."

Julie instantly regretted misleading her mother. Not only because she lied but she did not look forward to any pointers her mother might come up with. The only relief she had was that her mother was at least happy about it.

It was a really quick moment on her feet that had allowed her to come up with the happy couple cruise as an excuse for Byron, but excuses were getting harder to come by. Becky thought Byron was a vampire, except unlike vampires he didn't even come out at night.

Now, almost two years into their marriage, she wondered if marriage had simply changed the type of excuse she had to come up with. Before, it was excuses to avoid blind dates and weird men. Now it was excuses for why her husband couldn't come to parties or on double dates. Before, it was excuses to her mom about why she wasn't married and now it was excuses for why she wasn't pregnant.

I guess nothing is perfect, Julie thought, as she turned her wedding band in her hand.

Chapter 14

Popping the Question

The wedding was only two weeks away, and time had done a lousy job of making things better. Ms. Whitaker was still well on her way to becoming Mrs. Goodman and was reminding Byron daily of it. "You better not come up with some excuse why you and Julie can't be there at the last minute. It's only going to be the perfect wedding with you there."

"No. I'll be there," Byron promised.

He had repeated it so often that to make up something now would be impossible. He had left himself with no alternative, and with the day approaching he had decided that today was the day. He had blocked off an hour before lunch to make the phone call, but he was already fifteen minutes in and all he had done was stare at her contact information on his phone.

It was over two years since they had spoken. What would she think when he called?

He wasn't really sure what he was afraid of. What was the worst thing that could happen? The unknown was never easy for him to face and the more unknown the unknown was, the scarier it felt. But he was afraid for more reasons than that. He was afraid in part because he cared. He cared about Julie. And because he cared, not talking, not contacting, not knowing if she cared was better than reaching out and potentially removing all doubt.

He was about to call and ask a girl on a date. True it was his wife, which, under most circumstances, would increase the likelihood of receiving a positive response, but in his case, he wasn't so sure. As he stared down at the phone, the modern little rectangular box that did so much more than simply make phone calls changed in his memory to an old-fashioned telephone receiver, tan, and attached to a box on the wall with a long, curly, tan cord. He held the receiver in his hand and was staring at a scrap of paper with similar information, a name, and a phone number, Jennifer Wriggly, 343-5645.

Jennifer Wriggly had shared a freshman English class with him. Despite her obvious lack of ability in the subject, Byron had found himself favorably impressed by her. Jennifer definitely had it covered in the looks department. A tall blonde with long wavy hair, blue eyes, and very favorable shape, not that he would admit to noticing the last part, but while she looked great, what really drew Byron in was her confidence. *I could never be so blissfully unaware and so happy with myself,* he thought. But she was, and consequently had no trouble drawing in friends. Whatever self confidence you may lack, she could make up for. This was before graduate school, with its presentations and papers and all the academic praise. Silently sitting at the back of classes reaping in high grades was his strength, and he was happy doing it. So quietly he would sit, secretly, definitely not openly, not even in his own mind, envying her confidence.

Since leaving high school, coming to a new town, and having school to occupy his mind, he hadn't thought much about dating. However, with the winter ball approaching, his roommates couldn't seem to think of anything else. Day in and day out they pushed Byron to ask someone. "I'm too busy, and besides I don't have anyone to ask," was always his response. At first, he said it and meant it, but the more they spoke about it, the more he thought about it. And the more he thought about it, the more he realized there was someone, one girl, that he would love to go to the dance with.

The truth of the matter was, by the time he realized that he would love to go with Jennifer, it was way too late. There was only a week left until the dance and the chances that Jennifer had not been asked were so astronomical, actually by making some assumptions he had calculated it to be one in 149,000 chance. So, he decided to drop the idea, at least for that dance. The next dance would be a better opportunity.

The whole dance idea had left his mind until one day at the end of English class. Hoping to get some ideas on the next paper, he had stayed after to speak with the professor. While discussing the use of, or in his mind, overuse of asides in Shakespeare, he realized there was a book in the basket underneath Jennifer's seat. Suddenly asides were just that. He wrapped up his conversation with the professor and went to the desk and opened the book. It was manna from heaven, not only was the book Jennifer's, but she had left her full contact information in the front of the book and was requesting whoever might find the book to contact her. Jennifer was asking him to call her. Byron quickly wrote down the number, several times, on a scrap of paper with her name on it and placed the book in his backpack.

"Was that book left by a student?" the teacher broke his concentration.

"Yes."

"I can take it and bring it next time, if that would be easier for you."

"Oh, um, yeah, I guess that would be best."

The teacher had robbed him of his chance of calling Jennifer to return the book. He did have her number though, a prize he would hold onto for several months until the next dance when roommates again began to prod. Over those months, Byron debated over and over again if he should ask her to the dance, after all, even if he asked her before anyone else, she would probably say no.

After preparing for weeks, the day he had promised himself he would call arrived. It had to be early enough to ask before she was asked by anyone else, yet late enough that he didn't look crazy. So, there he was, receiver in his hand, staring down at the scrap of paper. Dialing was never such a difficult task. He started, stopped, messed up, started over but eventually the phone rang on the other side.

"Hello."

"Jennifer, this is Byron and I have something to ask you. See, in four weeks, the school will be putting on a dance and all of my roommates will be going to the dance, and since they are all going I thought, at least what I mean is . . . " He paused from the speedily prepared speech to breathe.

"Actually, this is Brittany, Jennifer's roommate, I can go get her."

"Oh . . . yeah, that would be great." Byron was glad this was a phone call so no one witnessed his whole face turn pink.

Jennifer came on and Byron ran the speech again without pauses.

"Who is this?" she questioned.

"I'm Byron. I'm in your English class."

"Well, um, Byron, I haven't even thought about the dance. I mean, I might be visiting home that weekend. I really don't know."

"Oh, yeah, of course, I shouldn't have asked so soon. I'm sorry about that." There followed a long pause.

"That's okay. I'll see you in English class, okay?"

"Yeah. I'll see you then."

He never followed up to find out if she was going home. She was in English class the Friday before, and he assumed she avoided any eye contact with him, but he couldn't be sure because he worked so hard to avoid it with her. Somehow, he felt if they made eye contact, she would have to officially turn him down. Since he never talked to Jennifer again and avoided all the talk of the dance, his eyes would even avoid any hallways lined with pictures from the dance. He would never find out if she went to the dance with someone else or not, and he wanted it that way.

After this, he would avoid his roommates for a few weeks before each dance, engrossing himself in his school. His freshman year was the only year he even had roommates and therefore Jennifer was the last time asking a girl out had been a serious thought, until today.

Here he was staring at a phone and contact information again. Who would have figured that when his crushed ego hung up that phone, it would take him fifteen years to pick it up again? He sat up in his desk, pulling himself out of his flashback, and went back to business. At least the dialing part sure had gotten easier over the years.

"Hello, Clark County Credit Union," the voice on the other line said brightly.

"Oh, excuse me. I thought this was Julie . . . must be a wrong number." He went to hang up the phone when he realized the "B" in the contact information he had saved, probably stood for bank. That way he would be able to get her new contact information for money transfer without having to speak with her. When he had switched phones, only some of his contacts transferred, clearly hers had been lost but he still had her bank. He quickly picked up the phone, "Are you still there?" he asked.

"Yes, sir."

"Well, I need the phone number for Julie Smith."

"Sir, this is a credit union."

"Yes, I know. She has an account with you."

"I'm sorry, sir. We can't give out personal information."

"No, you can. I mean, I'm on the account."

"Who am I speaking with?"

"This is Byron Lewis"

"And your relationship to Julie?"

"She's my wife."

"Your wife . . . ? And you need her phone number?" He was beginning to realize how ridiculous this sounded. He couldn't think of a good excuse, and the truth was the worst of them, so he went for the straightforward approach.

"Yes, I need her phone number."

"Just a minute, sir." The pause became belated enough he was beginning to think she wasn't getting the phone number.

"Hello, sir, this is the manager. What is it you need?"

"I need my wife's phone number."

"Sir, it is difficult to believe that being her husband you would need to acquire her phone number from us. Therefore, we will need to verify your identity." Next followed a lengthy conversation involving a social security number, birth date, mother's maiden name, first family pet, and the name of his first elementary school. All these he passed with flying colors, but then came the final question: "What day were you married?"

"Married?"

"Yes. Your anniversary."

"Right. Well, I know my anniversary," he slowly stated as he started scrolling through his calendar hoping he had his marriage written on there. "Well, it was two years ago . . . and it's currently 2008," he continued his slow speech.

The banker helped with the math, "So, it was 2006, sir. What day?"

"Oh . . . yeah . . . the day. Here it is! I mean . . . June 5th. That's it, June 5th, 2006."

"That's correct. You probably should have called us for her number a week ago." Byron looked at the calendar and realized it was June 9th, but he was growing tired of the banker's commentary. He knew asking a girl out wouldn't be easy, but this was worse than he had imagined. After the dreary inquisition, the banker gave Byron his wife's number. It was now a half hour later and he was no closer to having a date. His patience was wearing thin.

"Thank you, sir."

"Anytime you need your wife's number, just give us a call."

Despite how much Byron hated the banker making a joke at his expense, the sarcastic comment did ensure that the first thing Byron did was save the new number and note the first as belonging to the bank. He again picked up the phone, praying the banker had given him the correct number. If he went through anything else, he would spend his time coming up with an excuse for why his wife was, yet again, absent.

"Hello?"

"Hello, is this Julie?"

"Yes, who is this?"

"This is Byron."

"Who?"

"Byron Lewis. I'm your husband." The other end went silent and he heard muffled whispering.

"Oh, sorry, I couldn't hear you at first, we must have a bad connection. How are you doing, honey?" Wow, he hadn't expected such a warm welcome.

"Good," he cautiously responded.

"How has your day been?" she asked enthusiastically.

"My day? Well, it's been a good day. How was yours?"

"Oh, it was so good. You know, spending time shopping with Becky. I didn't expect you to call while you were in Alaska."

"Alaska?! What made you think I was in Alaska? I've never been to Alaska."

"So, you're enjoying your trip, then?"

"I'm not on a trip! I'm in town."

"Well, honey, I have to run, but I'll give you a call back when I get home around five."

"Five? . . . um, do you have my number?"

"Of course!"

"Five really isn't going to . . . " Byron attempted to say.

"Okay, I'll call you then. Love you! Bye." Before Byron could answer, the line went dead. That had to be the strangest phone call he had ever participated in. Had she heard him? He sensed she had but could make no sense of her responses. He was beginning to wonder if asking her was even worth it for a whole night of a conversation like that. Had she gone crazy in just two years? But he really needed to show up with her at an event. So, he better at least take her five o'clock phone call. He pushed for his secretary.

"Ms. Whitacker, do I have an appointment at five?"

"No, sir."

"Perfect."

Five o'clock came and Byron sat ready at his desk. At 5:10 he wondered if she was really going to call. By 5:15 his patience was wearing thin. *Why couldn't she talk to me when I called earlier?* he thought. After twenty minutes staring at the phone and debating in his mind if she was actually going to call, he thought he better occupy his mind with something else. He had several books he had started and hoped to get a chance to finish. He walked over to his bookshelf and picked one up. "How to manage time and be on time while having a wife." A book by his old professor. He laughed when he first read the title, but as clients with such issues began to stockpile, he decided he had better read it. Just as he opened to where he was in the book, the phone rang.

"Hello, this is Doctor Lewis," he replied.

"Hi Doctor, this is Julie." The voice on the other side sounded much less peppy and happy to speak with him then it had earlier today.

"Yes, hello, Julie. I thought you were going to call at five."

"I said about five . . . Anyways, why did you call? Is there something wrong?"

"No, I actually was wondering . . . well before I ask, what was the deal with Alaska?"

"Oh um . . . I was with somebody and I had told her . . . well, it doesn't matter. Basically, I didn't expect you to call and I was not in a good position to talk. If you had called at a better time, I wouldn't have said what I said," she said rather defensively.

"Well, I'm sorry, I didn't know there was a specific time I was supposed to call."

"Anyway, why did you call?"

"Oh yes, the reason I called was that I was hoping you would be able to . . . well, let me explain first." He paused for acceptance but none came, so he started to think of how he would explain. Nothing came to mind, so he simply stated, "See my secretary is getting married in a few weeks and I was wondering if you could come?" There was a long pause. "She has been planning this for months and she really wants you, I mean us, to be there."

"As long as you're there, why does she care if I'm there?" she said.

"It would be nice. It's getting hard to come up with excuses as to why you're not at these events."

"You think it's easy for me? Where do you think Alaska came from?"

"I understand, but this is big. It would be really nice if you could attend. I realize you have no obligation to attend as it is not part of our contract, but I would appreciate it." He had really hoped to avoid begging but it was looking like that was exactly where this was headed.

"My company threw a big ten-year anniversary that fell on my birthday, do you think it was easy to explain why my husband was, once again, not at the company party, and couldn't be with me . . . *on my birthday*? Did I call and beg you to come? No. I had to make up the story about Alaska."

"This is really important."

"Oh, my life's not? Just yours."

"I didn't say that," he said, more aggressively than he meant to.

"Don't get angry. You are the one who called and wanted to talk."

"You're right. I'm sure we can work something out." He paused for a moment to formulate his thoughts. "You come to my event, I will go to one of yours." Secretly he didn't really see this as fair but now wasn't the time to vocalize it.

"I'm not really sure I want you to come."

"I thought you were sick of making excuses?" Her grasp of logic seemed to be slipping.

"I am sick of making excuses, but I didn't say it was worth going to your events." There was a pause as he wondered what else he could possibly say. But before he made the huge mistake of offering her money, she said, "I'm kidding, I can come as long as you realize you owe me." You owe me was a little strong in his mind, so he made sure to clarify.

"You mean I will go with you to *one* of your events."

"Yes, that's what I mean. Why is everything a contract with you? Well, when is this big day of yours?"

"It's next Friday night at seven o'clock," he said, quite relieved to have the asking part out of the way.

"Friday will work for me."

"Good. Well, I will talk to you later then."

"Wait, where is it?"

Byron was so focused on getting her to say yes, he had completely forgotten about such details. "Sorry, of course you need the address, it is going to be at Lake Las Vegas. The party will be in their outdoor greenhouse. Do you need directions?"

"No, I can work Google as good as the next girl."

"Okay I will see you there then," he said, again trying to wrap up the call.

"Are we just going to meet there?" he heard as he began to hang up the phone.

He picked the phone back up, "Yeah, I thought that would be most convenient."

"So, you want your secretary to see that you do have a wife?"

"Yes," he paused. Hadn't they already established why she was attending? A recap of the call seemed unnecessary in his mind.

"And you want your secretary to think we are happily married?"

"Yes?"

"And we are going to come and go in separate cars?"

The line of questioning became crystal clear. "Good point." He hated to admit the questions that seemed so stupid led to something so smart. "We could meet in a nearby parking lot and then go from there."

"You know, it would be easier for me if you just picked me up."

"At your house?"

"Yes, at my house."

"Yeah, that's where you live." Wow he realized this phone call better end soon, it was not making him look too bright. "Yeah, I can pick you up. Where do you live?"

"I can text you my address."

"Perfect, I will see you then." He breathed a sigh of relief as he went to hang up the phone.

He paused to make sure she hung up first. He had imagined all he had to do was get her to say yes, little did he know you had to plan every detail before you called. With all that went into a date, he was beginning to be happy that it was a part of his life he was able to skip.

Chapter 15

The First Date

Byron pulled up to Julie's house exactly three minutes early at 6:27. Actually, he had been sitting in his car for over ten minutes about a block away because he didn't want to pull up too early. He had decided that three minutes early was about the perfect amount of time and now approached her house. The house was a perfect picture of suburbia. Like every house in Las Vegas, it had been built in the last few years, but unlike most Vegas homes, it didn't look exactly like every other one on the block. It had flower boxes at windows, a decorative vine arch over the entry, and a nice picket fence around the yard. It was clear that Julie had made considerable effort to make this place her own. Byron was a little embarrassed seeing her house. The only thing he had done to his house was slowly kill all his landscaping through neglect. Julie's thumb, and probably all her fingers, must have been greener than his.

He approached the fence with flowers in one hand and a corsage in the other. The fence was a short, white picket fence, and he decided stepping over the fence would be easier than trying to open it with his hands full. He put one leg over the fence. As his foot hit the ground and he was left straddling the fence, he realized this fence was a bit higher than he had expected. As he swung his other leg over the fence, the cuff of his pant leg caught the tip of a picket. He hopped in an effort to release his cuff. Quickly he realized that one limb was not enough to stabilize himself so leaning to one side, he dropped the flowers and his hand connected with the ground. With his stability regained, he jerked the cuff of his pant leg off the fence. Finally free, he put both feet firmly on the ground, and dusted himself off. Quite proud of having not fallen, that is until he looked up and there Julie stood on the porch.

"I didn't know we were going dancing," she said as she stepped off the porch and began to walk towards him. She stepped past him and reached for the gate. She flipped the latch and opened the gate. "Let me show you how this works."

He was far too embarrassed to make any remark on the incident. So he said all he could think of. "I got you these." He picked the flowers off the ground. Considering they had just been tossed several feet, they didn't look too bad.

"Thank you," she said with a grin.

"Oh, and I got you this." He pulled out the corsage from his pocket.

"You got me flowers *and* a corsage?" she asked.

"Is that bad?" Byron knew he had seen his roommates and friends in the past get flowers, and sometimes corsages for nice dates. Had they never been given together? He hadn't thought of it before.

"No, I guess it's not bad. I just never heard of getting both. Do you usually give a girl both?"

When it came to dating, Byron knew he had no "usual," but he thought now wasn't a good time to bring that up. "No, I mean not all dates. Just nice ones."

"Well, thank you. I guess," she said. As uncertain of her own sincerity as she was of his.

She looked up at him to see if he was going to put the slightly squashed corsage on her wrist, but since he was already headed to the car, she did it herself.

While he did not know etiquette about putting on her corsage, he did not fail in the "getting the door" department. He opened, she sat, and he closed. At least that part went smoothly. As he walked around the car, Julie was busy inspecting it. The leather interior felt good, and she was surprised to see the car was so clean. She had no idea what kind of car it was, but she guessed it was expensive.

He opened the door and got in, and before starting the car he asked, "Which tie should I wear?"

"Which tie?" she said, confused.

"Which tie?" he restated, gesturing to the back seat.

There she noticed the ten ties lining the back seat. As she looked, Byron noticed for the first time what she was wearing. He had been so embarrassed by the fence snag, and then so worried about the flowers and door, he hadn't noticed her dress. It was a light purple dress with short sleeves. It was long itself, rather modest, but a little form fitting, which, considering her form . . . he didn't mind. She turned to respond, he quickly turned away, trying to look like he had been inspecting ties.

"Why are you having me pick?" she asked.

"I wanted to match, us being married and all."

"Oh, I see." She looked over the ties and realized the answer to which one she would choose was "none of them." He may have good taste in cars, but definitely not ties. "Why not the red one?" she finally replied.

"Does red go with purple?"

"Um . . . sure."

He started the car and, after buckling up, began to drive away as he started to tie his tie.

Byron and Julie were both at a loss for words. What do you say to your spouse that you haven't seen in over two years? It was funny that when they were seeing each other every day planning the wedding, they had tons to talk about, but now they should have two years' worth of things to talk about and couldn't think of a thing.

"So, how have you been?"

"Good, you?"

"Good."

That was it. Silence draped over them as both were stuck in thought trying to think of what to say or talk about.

"Want to listen to the radio?" Julie asked.

"Sure."

And thus ended the conversation until they arrived at Lake Las Vegas, parked, and began to walk towards the pavilion where the wedding would be taking place. *If this entire night is going to be silent, it is going to be long indeed*, thought Byron. He sure hoped Ms. Whitaker would be happy about this. But, as they approached the wedding venue, the awkwardness between them lightened.

Dusk was just settling over the Las Vegas valley and, as it did, the heat of the sun dissipated to a perfectly cool evening. The lake glistened in the last flecks of sunlight and a subtle breeze drifted by. The grounds would have looked more at home in the gardens of an English countryside than a desert casino. Green grass, small bushes, and fountains adorned the grounds. As they got closer to where the ceremony was to take place, they noticed two rows of chairs that faced toward a beautiful waterfall. At the base of the waterfall stood an archway clearly set up for the wedding. Soft jazz played in the background. The surroundings began to seep into both their moods and they couldn't help but feel a sincere joy for being there. Byron looked over at Julie and realized that she added perfectly to the amazing setting. The last two years, which up to this moment he would have described as rather peachy, were now looking more like a waste. Why had he waited so long to see her?

"Julie."

"Yes, Byron."

"I'm glad you came."

"You know, I am too."

Small groups of people gathered throughout the grounds. It was still over a half an hour before the ceremony started so they felt no rush to sit down.

"I wonder how Mr. Goodman is doing?" Byron questioned.

"Who?"

"The groom."

"I am sure he is doing a lot better than you were on our wedding day."

"I sure hope so."

"Byron and Julie!" a voice called out from behind them. Turning around, Julie and Byron came face to face with Father Young. "How are you two?"

"Great," Julie got out. "What are you doing here?"

"I'm the lucky man performing the ceremony. We don't do them at the church anymore because we still haven't got the stains out." He looked over at Byron. "Just kidding, but we did have to replace that section of carpet."

"Sorry about that," Byron apologized, digging his hands into his pockets.

"I'm just happy to see you two. And glad to see you two together."

"Why? You thought we wouldn't make it?" Julie said.

"Not that at all. It's just that I like to keep up and help the couples I marry and I haven't had a chance to touch bases with you. So, I am glad we have this interview."

Interview? It was such an odd term for randomly running into each other. Byron didn't like the word choice or how he said it. "But it looks like we have enough time before the ceremony starts. If you will come this way, we can sit over on that bench."

Interview had been exactly what he meant. "Oh, Father, I think we better say hi to some of the other guests. Don't you think?" Byron said.

"No, plenty of time for that after the ceremony." And he herded them toward a small bench surrounded by some rather tall bushes. It was about as private as one could get in the area. Byron and Julie sat down. There wasn't room for anyone else as it was the closest Byron and Julie had ever been to each other and both felt pleasantly uncomfortable. Byron quickly surmised that Father Young had no intention of sitting, even if there had been room, as he peered down at them as he began the interview.

"So, how is the marriage?" Father Young asked with a smile, as casually as if he had asked them if they liked the weather today.

Byron looked at Julie, Julie looked at Byron. Neither of them wanted to tackle the question and was trying to convey to the other that they should take question one, but they had very little history on reading each other's cues. Finally, Byron spoke up. "The marriage? It's great."

Father Young's smile disappeared and his tone held a new note of seriousness as he asked, "How is the communication between you two?"

Again, they looked at one another.

"Oh, it's—" Byron started.

"Communication?" Julie started over Byron.

"Oh, sorry, you go."

"No, go ahead."

"No, you go ahead."

Byron made a zipping motion over his lips and pointed to Julie. She breathed deep, turned to Father Young and said, "The communication is great."

"I see. So, when was the last time you two got out on a date? I don't have to tell you, Byron, dating in marriage can be very important." Byron was beginning to see why some men in his office hated him so much.

Julie turned and flashed a slight smile at Byron and then, turning back to Father Young, said, "Father Young, you are so right." She then let her head tilt toward Byron again as she placed her hand on his knee. "Byron and I were just talking the other day that we need to get out together more often. That is why he asked that I drop the other commitments I had and come with him to this wedding." She turned and gave a look of perfect love, as if to show her admiration for him as she continued. "And we have decided next weekend to do something extra special." She turned back to Father Young as she closed with, "I am so glad we get to be at this wedding to remind us of the vows we took."

Two thoughts instantly went through Byron's head. The first was that he really liked her touching his knee. He knew it was part of the show for Father Young, but fake or not he couldn't help but like it. Second, Julie had missed her calling, there was no doubt she should have moved to LA and collected academy awards.

"I am glad to hear that," Father Young said, clearly pleased with Julie's performance. "Don't let it go too long between rekindling the romance. Well, I better get up to the front. Wish me luck, I never thought I needed it at these things until your wedding."

At first, Byron was extremely happy to see him walking away, but as soon as he was a few yards away, Julie moved her hand and Byron wanted to call out, "Come back." But he knew the act was up.

"You were amazing."

"Thank you," Julie accepted as she stood.

"That was award-winning. And I know. I have seen a lot of people try to fake happy marriages in front of me."

"I would like to thank the academy," Julie pretended to give her speech.

"How did you do it?"

"Father Young wanted to see we had a happy marriage and we do, don't we?"

"Ah . . . yeah . . . I . . . guess."

"I mean I am happy. Aren't you?"

Byron paused, "Yes. I am . . . happy. I guess."

"So, once I decided we are happily married, I knew I could do what Father Young wanted to see to get him off our backs."

"Well, my hat, if I had one, would be off to you. Shall we take our seats?"

They headed to the seats and, luckily for them, just in time. They had barely let their posterior hit the chair when the wedding march began. As Ms. Whitacker stepped into view, Byron couldn't help but think of the day he and Julie had married. He could hardly believe Julie had to walk down the aisle with him sitting on the pew looking like death itself. Remembering his vulnerable state, and thinking of her reviving him in the back office, brought a rush of emotions. He really did care about this crazy girl he called his wife. Looking over at her now, their eyes caught and he wondered if she was having the same thoughts, remembering that day. Did that horrible experience, which now brought him nothing but joy in hindsight, do the same for her? He would never have assumed so, but looking at her now, somehow he thought it might be possible.

Ten minutes later and Father Young was saying, "I now pronounce you husband and wife. You may now kiss the bride."

They stood and cheered as Julie leaned over to Byron. "Wow, no one even passed out."

"That's because they are doing food, drinks, and dancing afterwards. If I knew there was an eclair waiting for me after the ceremony, maybe I would have stayed conscious for it."

"Well, we can go get some now." But in doing so Julie had underestimated the passion for eclairs held by the Whitackers and Goodmans, before she could finish her sentence, the line for stuffed pastries had already overstuffed the small gazebo where the pastries were being held. "I guess we are going to have to wait a little longer on that eclair."

Music had once again started and there was a small dance floor. Byron may have never been a Casanova but the one thing he did know how to do was dance. "Do you want to dance?" he ventured.

"You dance?"

"A little. My mom forced me to take a class my freshman year of college."

"Forced?"

"I say, 'forced' to protect my manhood, but I may have enjoyed it."

Julie smiled and took his arm.

Byron took her hand in his, slowly put his arm around her back and pulled her in close as she put her arm on his shoulder. He led her in a short foxtrot, and she followed with ease.

"Want to learn a few more steps?"

"Sure."

"I think I remember a few steps." The first one he tried had a short lead in and then he twirled her 360 and then pulled her back into his arms in perfect rhythm back into the basic step. Moving in perfect step to the music was invigorating. As the song began to close, he spun her one last time, drew her in close, and they locked eyes as he dipped her back. He pulled her up as those around them clapped.

"You're a good dancer," Julie said.

"You're quite good yourself."

"I have a good teacher." By now quite a few couples had joined them on the dance floor, although most were simply swaying more than any official dance step.

The next song began to play. It was a waltz. "Do you know the waltz?" Byron asked.

"I'd really like to learn."

Standing more by her side then in dancing position, he showed her the 1-2-3, 1-2-3 required to do the steps. After a few times side by side, he pulled her to him, and they began to try it together. As the rhythm became a natural part of their movements, they moved in closer and closer until they were slowly moving together as Byron counted out 1-2-3, 1-2-3. He grew quieter and quieter as they drew closer and closer. Their cheeks met and they now silently moved, becoming one with the breeze and the music. Unfortunately, the music eventually stopped, and although neither of them wanted to stop, continuing to dance without the aid of a song was too socially unacceptable. The next song was not a fox trot, swing, or waltz but rather more of a jump up and down and yell song. Not being in Byron's repertoire, they left and began meandering towards a bench near the lake. Julie took his arm as they walked.

"Thanks, that was a lot of fun. I never thought I'd get a chance to dance. I mean, I have had chances to dance, but not really dance," Julie said.

"I know what you mean. I've always enjoyed it. But you don't get many chances to do real ballroom dancing anymore."

As soon as they got to the bench, Byron took a look back at the gazebo. The line had died down, so he decided it was time to answer the call of the eclair. "I'll go grab us a few goodies and punch."

Julie sat down and looked over the lake. It was perfect, really too perfect. She had never felt this way before. She found herself asking, *what changed?* She hadn't become rich or gotten a new job. Everything she thought meant something in her life was the same right now as it had been this morning, but she felt so different, so good. The realities of life didn't justify feeling this good, but she did. She was fairly confident that if she took a few steps out into the lake, she wouldn't get wet. She had never felt so light, so alive. It had been so long since she felt like this. And as she thought, she corrected herself. It hadn't been so long, because she had never felt quite like this. Perhaps she was under some sort of drug. But she couldn't be, she hadn't even tried the eclair or punch yet.

At times, putting a name to a feeling can be liberating and wonderful, but it can also have other effects. As soon as Julie realized what she was feeling was love, her mind took over and began to dominate a realm better left to the heart. *I am in love. I love my husband. That's good. But if I would have known how wonderful love was, would I have committed to marry someone without it?*

Her heart would have known how to handle this. It was ready to joyfully accept this wonderful twist of fate, but her mind was not as prepared. When we love someone, especially someone we don't know well, we become prone to self-doubt. Does he love me too? We ask.

In grade school this plays out with notes carried by liaisons that ask the person to circle yes or no below the words, "Do you like Julie?". But unfortunately, Julie didn't have anything to write on, and no one to take Byron the message. So, as Byron waited for his chance at the punch bowl behind Mrs. Goodman's four pudgy nephews, Julie began to ask, *What if Byron doesn't love me? After all, why would he. If he loved me, he wouldn't have waited two years to see me again. Yes, he danced with me, but he said he likes dancing. He probably would have liked dancing with Cinderella's stepsisters. No, what we have is purely a business deal. His caring for me was no more real than my act in front of Father Young. Of course, he would play nice and act friendly to me, but why wouldn't he? It was all part of the act.*

She could sense that the only thing more magical then the feeling she had would be feeling that way for someone and them feeling it in return. Because of Byron, that would forever be impossible. She had given up her chance at real love when she had committed to a marriage that was simply a business contract. Byron had gone from the man who gave her the magic, to the man who had robbed her of it forever, all while picking up an eclair.

"You should try these. They are amazing," Byron said, with no shortage of frosting on his lips. "I brought you some punch and two eclairs."

Julie turned and Byron was surprised to see tears in his wife's eyes. She tried to stop the tears as he spoke. "They're kind of small but . . . "

"I'd like to go home."

She could see that Byron didn't want to leave, but she couldn't stay and was grateful all he said was, "Okay." Walking back to the car, he dumped the punch and eclairs into a nearby trash can and they had a long, silent drive home.

Chapter 16

Meeting the Parents

The two weeks since Byron's secretary's wedding had come and gone, and tonight was Byron's turn to reciprocate. Julie had chosen to make Byron stay with her this weekend, since her parents were in town. Byron's only encounter with Julie's parents was on the day of their wedding and the thought of having to again see Pelham Smith made him quiver with fear. The promise Pelham had asked of him still rang in his head. He tried to forget it, and for much of the past two years he had been successful, but when he thought of again spending time with Pelham, the words came back as if he had heard them for the first time. "Promise me you will always put her first, care for her, and fight for her needs." Was Pelham going to ask for another interview and test how he was doing on this promise? What would he say? His experience was that most parents didn't get involved with their married daughters' personal life too much, but something in his gut made him worry that Pelham wasn't most parents. And the more he thought of spending time with his father-in-law, the more his stomach relived the churning from his wedding day. He had thought of backing out, but Julie had held up her end of the bargain. It was time for him to hold up his.

Byron showed up just in time to hide his luggage in her room before Julie's parents showed up. He decided pulling up with a packed suitcase was not a good look. Things all seemed to go fairly smoothly on the drive to the restaurant, during dinner, and the drive home. The conversation was mostly on sports, weather, and food options. The only heated debate came when Julie insisted it was perfectly appropriate to have tacos on a night that wasn't a Tuesday. Something her father could not abide.

"When God sends us a perfectly good alliteration like Taco Tuesday, it seems a mockery to be eating tacos on another night," Pelham argued, rather convincingly in Byron's mind. But Byron wisely chose to stay on the sidelines. It's never wise for the in-law to weigh in on deeply rooted family spats. So, the night seemed to roll along swimmingly.

"Good night," her parents called out as they walked down the hall. Julie opened the door to her bedroom and walked in. Byron stood in the doorway looking at Julie, trying to sense if he was supposed to follow. Julie, hoping to act before her parents looked back and noticed her husband looking like a puppy in the rain at the side door, grabbed his shirt and pulled him in, shutting the door behind them.

"I'm glad that is over with," Byron said.

"You're not the only one," replied Julie.

"Well, what now?" Byron questioned.

Byron got the same reply most husbands get to that question. "I'm going to bed."

Deciding he better get ready, Byron went to the closet where he had stored his bags. As he did, Julie went to her drawer and grabbed her night gown. He figured they would have to take turns changing in the bathroom but didn't want to tell Julie what to do. He'd watch her for clues but didn't want to look like he was watching her. So, Byron tried to not look, while looking. This maneuver is much like dunking a basketball. We all wish we could do it, but most simply can't. One of the difficulties in this is that looking while not looking requires so much looking that one fails to look where they are going and before Julie had done anything, he had tripped over his bag and laid sprawled out in front of her. She stopped, "You wouldn't fall if your bags weren't so big. Don't you ever travel?"

"I travel all the time, but not to strange woma—I mean, not to other people's homes," he said, catching himself in the nick of time.

"So, what did you need at my house that you wouldn't need when you regularly travel? Do you have a baseball bat to protect you from this strange woman?"

"I will have you know that I came prepared to keep proper boundaries."

"So, you brought 2x4's and some sheetrock to build a wall?"

Byron was getting irritated, mostly because he now felt dumb for bringing as much as he had, but he could easily blame her for not telling him he didn't need it. He decided not to comment but rather began preparing for bed. As he unzipped his bag, Julie caught sight of what had made his bag so large. Inside was a small tent and a sleeping bag.

"What is the tent for?"

"I thought you might want me to sleep outside."

"Did I say my parents were blind?"

"Excuse me?"

"You thought they wouldn't notice a tent in the backyard?"

Byron now felt even dumber. He realized his tent idea over-looked Julie's parents' perceptiveness and general ability to see, but why should he be taken to task for being thoughtful? This hurt Byron deeply, mostly because as he had packed the tent, he imagined Julie seeing him unpacking it and saying, "Oh what a sensitive man. You care enough about me to rough it on the hard ground with no A/C in the middle of the summer. You are truly my knight in shining armor." He wouldn't admit to wanting to be Julie's knight in any tint of armor, but he wouldn't have minded some gratitude and maybe a little fawning.

On top of this, Byron felt a significant blow to his self esteem. It reminded him in sixth grade when he had entered a bridge building competition. At that point in his life, he had planned to become an engineer and, looking at his bridge, he knew he had made the right choice. It was a magnificent bridge. The two trusses on each end were beautiful. It was bound to be the strongest bridge in the competition. The judge took his bridge and carefully placed it under the piston that would slowly apply pressure to it until it was crushed. Byron hated to see his beautiful bridge getting crushed but was sure it would come with the glory of having held the most weight in the class. The piston slowly began to descend when suddenly the judge sneezed and all the kids knew exactly what had happened to the first little pigs home. The judge swept the sticks into his hands and said, "Sorry, son. Next."

Byron always thought he had keen ability to understand the fairer sex even if no one from the fairer sex agreed. He felt hurt that when his perceived strength was put to the test, he was again left holding the broken pieces. Originally when packing, he had thought, *If only the men who came to me were as thoughtful as I am, they wouldn't need my help.* His wounded pride now was thinking what most men in his office thought, "I bet most women would appreciate my thought-fulness." But rather than voice this, he simply said, "What sleeping arrangements did you have in mind?"

She hadn't really thought too much about it because she figured it didn't need to be that hard. "You can sleep on the floor and can use the extra blanket, or your sleeping bag since you have it. And to ensure you feel proper, I will go change in the bathroom," she said as she took her pj's and headed into the master bath, shutting the door harder than she had meant to.

Byron took his blanket and headed downstairs to the living room couch. Neither party really wanted it this way, but Byron knew from many interviews that the couch was the customary location for wounded husbands. So, he stretched out on the couch that he almost fit in. He went over the last five minutes in his head, one hundred times, trying to think what advice he'd give, if he ever came to himself, literally, and more importantly, what advice he'd give Julie. He finally gave up and forced himself to sleep.

Julie stepped out of the bathroom only to discover that the one day her husband had been home had come to an early end. She too was upset that Byron had left and wished she hadn't been so sarcastic or poked fun at his tent and sleeping bag, after all, it was for her. Secretly, she was sarcastic because it helped her stay in control, not allowing herself to be vulnerable, and therefore not get hurt. But all this avoiding getting hurt was starting to hurt. A few tears hit her pillow as she too forced herself to sleep.

Byron slowly turned over and began to open his eyes. He had forgotten he was laying on his wife's couch, having spent the night before in his first official marital argument, but the stiff neck and tight muscles quickly told him he was not in his bed. As he gathered in his surrounding and his memories fell back into place, he realized he was not alone in the living room. Directly across from him in the large lazy boy sat his father-in-law, holding a magazine, but looking down at Byron.

"Good morning, Byron."

"Oh, good morning," Byron was so embarrassed about having his father-in-law see him sleeping on the couch that he quickly tried to come up with an excuse. "Oh, I couldn't sleep last night so I came down to get something to eat and must have fallen asleep before I got to the fridge," he managed to stammer.

"It's okay, Byron. You think I never ended up on the couch? Even marriage counselors don't have perfect marriages, right?"

"Yeah, I guess not," Byron said. "But honestly, this is the first time I have spent the night on the couch."

"I believe you. Hey, do you mind showing me what I could have for breakfast?" he said walking towards the kitchen.

Byron didn't like the question, actually it wasn't the question as much as how the question was asked. Pelham was up to something. "Yeah, sounds good," he said, following him.

"So, do you have any cereal?" Byron's eyes quickly scanned the kitchen hoping to quickly find the cereal, but it wasn't on the counter or over the fridge, and Julie's cupboards weren't those cupboards made with glass doors. Byron had always thought glass door cupboards were such a stupid idea. Who wants to see inside your cupboards? Now he knew. Knowing he would only get one guess without looking like an idiot, he reasoned which cupboard would be the logical place to put the cereal. He made his choice and opened the large cupboard directly in front of where he stood. He smiled, fortune was on his side. There in plain view sat a few boxes of cereal.

"Well, Dad, what would you like? We have Special K, Cheerios, and Captain Crunch with Crunch Berries." Really, she had Captain Crunch? He didn't think people without kids were allowed to buy that. Now that he knew you could get away with it, he made a mental note to go and buy some.

"I'll have Special K. Where are the bowls and spoons?"

"Bowl and spoons? Yeah, you're going to need those." Byron stalled trying to mask the fact that he needed time to think. Where would he put the bowls and silverware? He had been right before. He went to the next cupboard and sure enough there were the bowls. This was going great. He handed his dad the bowl and if he got the spoons in his first guess, he would officially have three miracles and could apply for sainthood.

But the devil's advocate inside him calmly brought up that the last was the most difficult. Had anyone ever guessed the silverware drawer on their first guess? So many silverware sized drawers. Byron guessed, opening the small size drawer next to the sink. It revealed oven mitts. "Oh, I always forget, we had the silverware drawer here when I first moved here but we changed it." He went to option two, measuring cups, then spatulas, he could forget about that sainthood. Next was an empty drawer and placemats. *Who still has placemats?* he thought. At last he found silverware. "Here you go. You know Julie, can never make up her mind where to put things. I swear it's a new drawer everyday." His forced smile was not reciprocated by his father-in-law. Byron tried to move on. "Let me get you some milk." *At least I'll know where that is,* Byron thought as he opened the fridge. He looked around, no milk.

"Sorry, Dad, we must be out of milk. Although we do have soy milk." Muttering under his breath he added, "Heaven knows why."

"Why do you have soy milk?" asked Dad.

"You don't like the stuff either, huh?" Byron knew he liked this guy. "I keep telling Julie it's not that much healthier, but she won't listen, just keeps buying soy."

With a stern look, Pelham said, "My daughter is lactose intolerant."

Byron fell instantly silent, his mind quickly spun through anyway he could explain having said what he had just said, but nothing came to mind, so he took his shocked look, exaggerated it, and said, "If only she would have told me."

"Come on, Byron, the games up. What's going on with you and Julie?"

Byron didn't know what to say, perhaps pretend he was gone for the last month or so, and Julie had moved things, or say they had a few issues and were living apart, but none of that explained why he didn't know his wife of two years was lactose intolerant. Trying to explain that you are happily married, even though you live separately and never see each other, can be difficult. So rather than try, he turned it back to good old dad. "What are you talking about?"

"What am I talking about?" The question was repeated in such a way as to say you know exactly what I am talking about, but if you want me to spell it out for you I will. And spell he did. "You look as if you have never entered this house. You know where nothing is. The rooms, the lawn, the garage show no signs of a man. The only tools in the shed are a set of pink screwdrivers and crescent wrench we got Julie three years ago. Your cable subscription doesn't even include ESPN."

"It doesn't?" Byron said in shock.

Pelham picked right back up. "The bathrooms are full of Better Homes and Gardens, Martha Stewart, and Vogue magazines. There are far too many throw pillows, covered in far too many flowers. Which I'll admit is a plague most men can't stop. But look at this bookcase," he said as he walked back into the living room where a bookcase stood on either side of the entertainment center. "A few romance novels, some of Julie's college books, some Jane Austen's. But here you are with a doctorate and I can't find one book on counseling, psychology, or marriage and family therapy."

Pelham was right. The game was up, but just to ice any chance Byron thought he might have had of getting out of this, Pelham added, "In fact, haven't you written some books?"

The pause was pregnant, delivered a baby, and raised it by the time Byron finally said, "Yes."

"Can I see one?"

Byron had thought of bringing one of his books. Not fake bookshelf material, but rather a gift for his in-laws but then thought a book titled, "Your last chance: Saving a wrecked marriage even when your man seems like trash," didn't seem appropriate. But if only he had brought it, he could have pulled it out now, knowing that even if he did have it, it would have been like pulling out his supersoaker to try to stop a forest fire.

The pause was now having twins but Pelham remained silent, Byron was so unsure what to do he actually debated telling the truth, when Pelham finally said, "All right, son. Since I can tell this might be a long story, how about you and I go out and discuss it over breakfast. I'll go tell Julie and Barbara."

Pelham ran upstairs and, although it was muffled, Byron could hear most of it.

"Julie, Byron and myself are going to run out to get a bite to eat."

"He's here?"

"You sound surprised, why wouldn't he be here?"

From the tone, Byron could tell that Pelham enjoyed catching them in this lie.

"Well, I thought," Julie stammered out. "That he had to go into work this morning."

"No, he is very much here and I thought we could go have some male bonding over bacon and syrup. Tell your mother where we have gone, minus the bacon and syrup part, if she wakes up."

Byron suddenly realized he could have just made a run for it when Pelham went upstairs, but unfortunately the thought didn't enter his head until Pelham was headed back down. All he could do was take a deep breath and hope this interview went better than the one two years ago, but Byron saw little chance of that.

"Shall we?" Pelham said, opening the front door.

Chapter 17

The Challenge

"Well, Pelham," Byron was preparing to get it all out as they sat in the little booth at the diner.

"You can wait until we order to tell the story. I don't want to rush you," Pelham said

This helped Byron relax a little. The long, silent drive there hadn't set Byron at ease. He wondered what Pelham was going to say once he knew the whole truth, but Byron took solace in the fact that so far, he didn't sense any anger or judgment in his father-in-law's voice. Despite not being very hungry, Byron ordered a standard American breakfast—two pancakes, two eggs, and some bacon. At a diner for breakfast that is what you were supposed to order. Pelham on the other hand had his own idea. "I'll take eight pieces of bacon covered in maple syrup."

Byron was a bit surprised. Pelham looked about 100 pounds shy of a man who regularly ordered in this fashion. Also, last night he had not only ordered a salad but asked for dressing on the side saying, "They always put too much dressing, gotta watch those calories."

Pelham, noting the surprise in Byron's eyes, explained, "Byron, I realized a long time ago that I love two breakfast items, bacon and maple syrup. I also learned a long time ago that keeping my wife happy brings me more joy than what I eat. So, I eat what she wants me to eat when we are together and on the rare occasions I eat out without her, I eat what I want to eat. It's kept me both married and from turning into a blimp. Win-win. But we didn't come to this meal to talk about my marriage. We are here to talk about your's. So, lay it on me."

"Well." Byron took a deep breath. "I needed a wife."

"And why is that?"

"I thought it necessary mostly because some lesser-minded people found it hard to take me seriously as a marriage counselor without one."

"Always a good idea to allow lesser-minded people to dictate our decisions." Byron began to mutter an excuse, but Pelham encouraged, "Go on."

"So, I took an ad in the paper asking for a wife."

"I hope you kept a copy."

"What?"

"Scrapbook material."

"I suppose." This was not going at all as Byron had envisioned. Mostly it was going better. He wasn't sure he liked it. "Anyway, I received several answers but mostly people desperate for my citizenship, or my money. I almost gave up but one of the replies was from Julie."

"Kind of romantic."

Byron wasn't sure if that was sarcasm or not, so he kept going.

"Julie said she was tired of the dating scene and being pressured by . . . " Byron paused, catching himself before he said, "her mother," and instead said, "others, who thought she should be married."

"No reason to sugar coat it for me. You think I didn't notice Barbara calling everyday? I kept telling her that Julie wasn't going to meet someone and get engaged in one day, but it sounds like you might have proved me wrong on that count. Did you get engaged on the first day you met?"

"Um . . . yeah, we did."

"Well, I hope Barbara never finds out. I hate being proved wrong. But I digress, go on."

"We decided it would help both of us if we got married, so as you know, we did. After the ceremony, we went our separate ways."

"So, you have been totally separate from that day until this?"

"She did come with me to my secretary's wedding a few weeks ago because my secretary kept begging me to bring my wife. To pay Julie back I agreed to be here this weekend when you came to town."

"I see, so you married my daughter simply to further your career?"

"I don't know that I would say, 'simply.'"

"Okay. You married my daughter to further your career."

Byron realized this did not help his cause. To hear it stated so frankly, by the man who had trusted him with his daughter, was painful, and he sat looking like a dejected heap, not too different from the breakfast plate in front of him. Finally, in an effort to placate his sense of decency, Byron offered, "It was a crazy idea, I should have never done it. But we can get divorced and make things go back to how they were."

"What?" Pelham shot back so quickly that Byron knew whatever the correct answer was, this was not it. "That ranks up there with your stupid, let me run an ad in the paper to get a wife idea. Do you think I want to explain all this to Barbara and have to start to hear her complain about Julie's dating or lack thereof day and night again? I'd sooner admit to her that I just ordered seven strips of bacon smothered in syrup."

With this unexpected response, Byron felt like his most feared enemy had become his strongest ally.

"No, we must come up with a plan. We mustn't go back to how things were. The phone calls constantly asking Julie if she is going to have kids is bad enough."

"Kids?" Byron coughed up the only bite of egg he had managed to take. "She asks about kids? What does Julie say?"

"You two are 'trying,' but clearly not too hard. So, we can remove divorce as an option, what's your next idea?"

Byron didn't have any other ideas. Thinking about it, he was leaning towards leaving things as they were, but he doubted that Pelham would find that much more appealing than divorce. As he tried to see any other possible options, he suddenly realized he was in a marriage counseling session, only seated on the wrong side of the table. The realization came with the voices of hundreds of clients who had said to him, "Stay together and leave things as they are, or get divorced, what other choices are there?" He always viewed this as terribly closed minded, but somehow when it was his situation it didn't seem like such a terribly closed-minded thought.

When he counseled others, he always told them that there were hundreds of other options besides those two, and all of them involved the same thing: change. The options they didn't want to see or think about were the options that would force them to change. He now realized that Pelham was looking for an option that would force him to change.

He thought of all the magic moments in his office when the clients realized that he wasn't the type of doctor that simply asked them to pop a pill and pay the bill. No, he expected them to do real work, the hardest work anyone can do: change, to become a better person. This realization, at first, always led to the same thing: excuses. And Byron was no different. While he was too scared to vocalize the excuses, his mind was fabricating them with such efficiency that even Henry Ford would have been proud. *Why should I change? I'm not unhappy with our marriage. Julie isn't unhappy. I can't afford to change, changing would cost so much. I have no time, no energy, no money . . . no way.*

He looked up again at Pelham. Weighing in his mind which excuse was best but ultimately said, "What would you suggest?"

Byron had always wondered why his clients took so long to give him even brief responses.

"Well, I think a happily married couple should see each other more than twice every couple of years. Don't you?"

"I guess," Byron could see where this was going. "How often were you thinking?"

"We aren't haggling over a used car. How often, in your professional opinion, should a happily married couple see each other."

That sly dog, thought Byron. He always felt he was the master of asking the right question but he now realized he was but a novice compared to the great Pelham. But two could play at this game, "I have seen military couples have decent marriages who very rarely saw each other." This wasn't really true, but Byron assumed there must at least be one out there.

"Fair enough, but would you say at least twice a month is good for anyone not deployed overseas?"

"I guess so."

"So, how often are you going to see Julie?"

Byron had learned a long time ago that it was safe to simply repeat the professor. "Twice a month?"

"Sounds good to me. So, it's agreed you will go out with Julie at least once every other week. Feel free to call me and keep me up to date with how things are going."

Byron wanted to complain. He wasn't sure he had actually agreed to anything but as Pelham grabbed the last piece of bacon with a smile, Byron could see that the negotiation was closed. "Boy, oh boy. Six slices of bacon can really fill a man up," Pelham said as he sat back in his chair.

"I'm going to have a difficult time explaining to Julie that her dad is requiring us to date."

"That is exactly why I recommend you don't do that."

"What?"

"Son, this will work a lot better if Julie doesn't know that I know. Best to leave me out of it."

Byron felt like Pelham had just orchestrated D-Day and finished the inspiring speech with, "You boys have fun, I'll be waiting back in the US to hear how things went."

"So, what do I tell her?"

"I don't know. She's your wife. But if you really want a place to start, when I want to spend time with Barbara, I usually try something like, 'Hey babe, want to go see a movie?' or 'Honey, want to try that new Italian restaurant?' but you are smart, you can come up with your own lines."

Byron was still in a state of shock trying to process exactly what he had agreed to do and at this point if he could get out of it, when Pelham got up and said, "Well, we better go, but I am sure glad we had this chat. I think you'll do great, son."

Hearing Pelham call him his son was equally awkward for both men, but Byron knew he did it with the best of intentions, and it did serve to trip up his train of thought. While Byron appreciated the gesture, he wasn't sure he could reciprocate.

The ride home was as strange as everything else but only because it was normal. Pelham acted as if their conversation at the restaurant had never happened. He asked Byron about his work and Byron answered in short but responsive answers. Yes, Pelham was back to just being the same old guy. Byron on the other hand was anyone but his usual self.

His body may have been in the car but his mind was still sitting in the diner. All he was thinking about is what he was going to do and, worse, what he was going to say to Julie.

Byron was grateful that Pelham more than kept up his half of the conversation, because he was too busy mulling over what to tell Julie. He had seen so many men stew over the right words to tell their spouse, and for the first time, he was beginning to understand how they felt.

No sooner had Pelham opened the door than Julie jumped up from the couch, alert and ready to question them about this "bonding time." The anxiety of her unsuspecting husband unsupervised with her wily father had clearly been wearing on her.

"Oh, I'm glad you two are back," she said with a smile. "So, dear," she said looking at Byron, "What did you two talk about?"

Pelham, knowing that Byron was in no shape to be regurgitating full truths, let alone clever part ones, jumped in. "Darling, this husband of yours is quite the guy. He told me all about . . . " He went on to make their ten-minute car ride home, most of which Byron was comatose for, sound like a deep, two-hour conversation all about Byron's life. Pelham did have to make up quite a bit of it but did so knowing that Julie was unlikely to know any better.

It was clear Pelham was not only a great marriage counselor and negotiator but also quite the actor. By the end of his tale, Julie's nerves were visibly calmed, so much so that she gave Byron an unexpected but very welcome smile as a way to say, "nice work." It was a look he desperately wished he deserved.

"Well, I hate to admit this, but, honey, we better get our bags packed and get to the airport, we don't want to miss our flight," Pelham said.

"Do you need help with your bags?" Byron asked.

"Oh, we will take a half hour or so to pack. Why don't you two do whatever you do with your Saturday mornings? Julie told us how much you two love to garden together. Why don't you plant a few daisies? You can help me with the luggage once we have it all packed up."

Byron gave Julie a confused look and then together they headed out to the yard.

"Pelham, honey, Julie never told me Byron liked to garden," Barbara said, "And our bags are already packed."

"I know," he smiled as he looked out the window seeing Byron and Julie headed toward the small garden shed together. "Let's go take a nap."

The ploy to force them to spend time together didn't help much. Byron and Julie did go out to the garage, but Byron was so distracted with trying to figure out how he could meet his commitment he had made to Pelham that he made a terrible conversationalist. By the time they went back to say goodbyes, Byron was no closer to solving his problem.

The goodbyes on the front porch would have made Leave it to Beaver proud. Everyone was smiling and hugging and, most concerning to Byron, talking about how they needed to do it again soon. As Pelham went to hug Byron he whispered, "Make me proud, son."

"We will see you two love birds later," Barbara said as she walked to the car. Clearly less observant than Pelham, she saw exactly what she wanted to see and that was that their daughter was happy and, perhaps more important in her mind, happily married.

Byron and Julie continued to wave as Pelham and Barbara drove off. When they were safely away, Julie was the first to break the silence. "You can relax, you did great, you convinced them. I don't know how, walking around like a ghost all day, but you did it. Now that they are convinced, we won't have to see each other for a long time."

This was not the opening Byron wanted but it was an opening nonetheless. "Julie, maybe we should see each other more often," Byron slowly let out.

Byron could see the shock in her eyes. Her look seemed to ask if he were joking. He tried to convey that he was not, without trying to look desperate.

She quickly said, "Why?"

Byron wasn't sure what to say. He hadn't expected her to ask that. Come to think of it, he wasn't sure what he had expected her to ask. But, as he debated, the moment grew awkward.

She broke the silence by saying with a smile, "I said it went well, not *that* well."

Byron had hoped for a little more positive response, but the sarcasm was sufficient to let him know that it wasn't a total no. "I was thinking, perhaps, it would benefit both of us. We wouldn't need to come up with excuses so often. You could come on the double dates Ms. Whitaker, I mean Mrs. Goodman, is always bugging me about and I could come . . . "

"To my book clubs," Julie jumped in.

"Yes, I could come to your book clubs."

"So we will trade off. I go to one for you and you go to one for me, another business arrangement," Julie said with a little disappointment.

"You could call it that," Byron went on.

While void of any romance, Julie saw that this made sense. "So, what are you thinking, twice a year?"

"A little more than that might be nice. Maybe a couple times a month."

"That seems like a lot, to go from not seeing each other in years to now several times a month. Are you sure you don't want to do it only once a month? I mean, how often do you think book clubs meet?"

Byron didn't want to have to tell good old dad he had failed, so he stuck to it. "I think twice a month would be good."

"If you insist. But I go first. I have a book club coming up."

Byron couldn't believe it. It had worked. She had accepted. Ever since he had committed to dear old dad that he would see Julie twice a month, he had been completely stressed about her response to such a sudden change. With her acceptance behind him, he was absolutely elated. "Perfect, you let me know when that book club is and I will be there with bells on."

"What does that mean?"

"You know, it's a phrase, with bells on."

"I haven't heard it."

"Everybody's heard it."

"Not me. What does it mean?"

"You know, I'm not sure but I think it means you're excited to go or something like that."

"You're excited to go to my book club?"

Byron now realized he might have overplayed his excitement. "Well, I will be there. I'm not sure about the bells."

After this, Byron went back up to Julie's room and grabbed his lumbering suitcase full of things he never used. The entire time he kept his pep in his step.

Julie finally asked as they headed out the front door with his luggage, "Byron, what has gotten into you? You were a zombie throughout most of my parents' stay and now you are like a kid on Halloween."

"I guess I was so stressed about really getting to know your parents and I'm glad that it wasn't a total bomb. At least I hope you don't think it was."

"No, it seemed to go really well. Thanks for doing it."

"Well text me all the info on the book club. It will be interesting. I've never been to a book club."

"You'll enjoy it more if you actually read the book. Here, I finished it, you can borrow my copy." She handed him a book with a bright pink cover with an illustration of a bouquet of flowers on it and the title "The Husband Hunt."

"Is this a joke?"

"You said you would be there."

"And I will. I just hope no one sees me with that book. Well, I'll see you then."

They both kind of stood there not really knowing how to say, "See you later." End of dates are always a little awkward, neither party knows how far the other wants them to go. Should you just say, "Well, toodles," and hop in the car? Do you shake hands? Finally, Byron awkwardly leaned in and did a side hug. "Okay, I better get going."

"Bye, Byron," Julie said.

Did she want more than a side hug? Byron couldn't tell and he wasn't going to push his luck. Maybe next time. As he drove off, he noticed something about Julie in the rear-view mirror. She was beautiful, especially when she was smiling.

Chapter 18

Just Friends

The doorbell rang exactly at 5:45 p.m. Byron stood in the doorway in slacks, button up, and tie.

"Aren't you a little over dressed for a book club?" Julie asked.

"I don't know. Like I told you, I've never been to one."

"Well, you look nice," she said as they headed for the car. "Did you read the book?"

"I did," he said as he opened her car door.

Once he had come around and gotten in, she asked, "Well?"

"Well, what?"

"Did you like it?"

He smiled. "I'm not sure I'd use a strong word like, 'like.'"

"Okay then did you at least not hate the book?"

"Yes, I very much did not hate the book."

"Wait a minute," she said, peering into the back seat. "Is this the book?" She reached back and picked up a book that had a crudely made book sleeve over it, made from a brown paper bag.

"Yes, they made us do that to our textbooks in the seventh grade, a skill I never thought I would need again but it came in quite handy."

"You remembered how to do that from the seventh grade?"

"YouTube might have helped a little."

"I can't believe you were so scared of being seen with a pink-covered book that you made a cover for it."

"It did say in big letters, 'The Husband Hunt.' And it had nothing to do with embarrassment. It was because I wanted to protect your book."

"Yeah right," Julie said with a laugh. "Well, despite your fear of its cover, I'm sure you have to admit that the plot was kind of clever. I mean, I would have never thought to reunite four old friends at a high school reunion, all desperate and single, and have them make a bet that whoever gets married first gets their wedding paid for. That was a fun premise."

"Fun? I would say more farfetched," Byron said.

"What?" Julie said in surprise.

"I mean are you really going to bet with a bunch of friends to see who gets married first?"

"I can't believe you of all people think that it is far-fetched."

"Why me, of all people?"

"The guy who found his wife from putting an ad in the paper can't believe in a strange way for people to find their spouse."

The back and forth continued as they talked about what they liked or disliked about the various characters and the interactions and relationships that followed. Julie was a little disappointed when they came to Becky's house and knew that their conversation was over. She would have rather just talked to Byron about the book, but in they went.

Becky came to the door. "This is the elusive Byron. Glad you came out of hiding and finally joined us."

"You be nice to him or he will never want to come back," Julie chided her friend.

"I'm always the pinnacle of kindness," Becky said.

"Yeah . . . right," Julie countered.

"I am just so glad to see you again. I wondered if after the wedding Julie had secretly killed you and buried you in the backyard under her newly poured deck, only to be found out when they need a new episode of cold case files. After all, she had chewed up and spit out so many of the men I set her up with. Then out of nowhere you appear and convince her you are the one in a few weeks. But now that I know she just didn't kill you for your money, I really think you must be a magician."

"Okay, that is enough," Julie responded before Becky could get any response from Byron. They made it the rest of the way into the living room where four couples were all waiting and were introduced to Byron. Byron quickly saw why Julie wanted him to come along to this thing. For her to be the lone single with four couples while they talked about romantic novels was what Webster's would list under "awkward." Byron was surprised she kept coming at all and was even more surprised at how supportive these husbands were.

His amazement diminished as he quickly found out that the other husband's attendance wasn't much more frequent than his own, and as one by one they admitted that they had not read the book. Becky's husband was the last before Byron and he said, "Sorry, I didn't even pick it up."

Julie, with pride and to Byron's embarrassment, said, "Byron read it. And even admitted to not hating it."

Each of the wives glanced over at their husband to make it clear that they had fallen below the bar, and each husband wished Byron had been absent at least one more time. "Well at least one of our husbands cares," One of the daring wives blurted out.

Byron took the opportunity to fill his mouth with a cracker with some sort of cheese dip on it.

"I am very glad Byron read it," Becky said. "As a marriage counselor his insights will be most interesting."

"You're a marriage counselor?" one of the husbands asked in the same tone he might have asked, "Was it you with the wrench in the library?"

"Yes," Byron said as he felt any credibility he had with the men in the room evaporate. "But, I don't know that I have any special insights in this book." *After all,* Byron thought, *this wasn't exactly a textbook on a successful marriage.*

"But what about Amelia and Steve's marriage? Do you think it was right for them to divorce in the first place? Do you think you could have saved their marriage?"

"I don't know that it really makes sense for me to comment on the strength of a made-up character's marriage."

"Oh, come on. With them made up, what will it hurt?"

Byron really wanted to avoid any of this but he didn't want to embarrass Julie who was clearly saying with her look, "Come on, Byron. Answer their questions." So, despite the little voice inside his head telling him not to, he went ahead and said, "It was clear from how she wrote about Steve that he had depression he needed to deal with, and if he had dealt with it appropriately, he could have saved his marriage."

Byron could now hear the voice inside his head again as all the women in the room except Julie each tried to ask him a specific marriage question from the book all at once, it was saying, "I told you so."

The youngest of the group finally pushed the others down enough to get her question front and center. "So Byron, when Dolphin's man was so kind to her despite her attitude, didn't you just want to stand up and shout at all the men you meet and say, 'that is how you should treat a woman, even if she may not be in the best mood or not acting her best'?" Byron could tell that this question had nothing to do with the book.

This was made clear when her husband said, "She, whomever the woman was in the book, shouldn't expect to be treated any better than she treats him."

The next hour was spent dancing around marriage questions thinly veiled as questions about the book. The husbands were less careful. Likely since they hadn't read the book and couldn't veil their retorts.

Luckily, dancing was something Byron was very good at, and he actually felt that he handled it as well as anyone could expect, at least he hoped as well as Julie expected, that is until someone asked, "How long is the right amount of time to date before you marry?"

Byron was well equipped for this one. He was very strong both in the research of this question and his experience with couples matched what the research showed.

"You should date each other for a least a year before you commit to marriage, if you want to have your best chance at a successful marriage."

"One year. Didn't you and Julie get married after only a few weeks?"

"Well . . . um . . . a . . . with Julie and I things were different."

This was the exact opening the poor abused men in the room had been waiting for. "Sure, all this stuff seems like a good idea or easy to do until it's your marriage and then things are 'different'."

Byron did not appreciate the man's artistic choice to use air quotes around the word different.

"So, why were you two so different?" Becky asked. "How did someone who says you should wait at least a year decide a few weeks was enough?"

Byron didn't know what to say, and in desperation he looked over at Julie.

She smiled at him and jumped in. "Actually, he wanted to get married the day we met."

Everyone gasped as one of the husbands noted, "Mr. Marriage plays by his own rules," and Byron regained a tiny bit of respect from the portion of the group with more testosterone.

"Okay, let's talk about something else," Byron offered.

"Can't handle the heat when it's focus turns to your relationship, huh?"

"So, tell us Mrs. Marriage Counselor, what is it like to be married to a guy who is an expert on all things marriage?"

Julie didn't think this would turn back on her. But with everyone quietly waiting for a response, she simply did her best. "Byron's great in that he never really brings his work home with him."

And with that perfectly boring response, everyone moved on. Byron was happy to hear the next book that was picked had absolutely nothing to do with dating or marriage.

They ate a few more crackers and started for home.

"You did great in there," Julie told him as soon as they got to the car.

"Thanks. Do you ever read any books on civil engineering so we can ask you all the questions?"

"Nope, but don't worry, dating and marriage is only the focus of about 90% of what we read."

"Very comforting."

The drive home was even more fun than the drive there. Julie was once again enjoying herself. She was feeling the same magic she had felt at Mrs. Goodwin's wedding but this time she believed that it wasn't just business or for show. Byron was making an attempt to spend time and get to know her, and the more she got to know, the more she liked. Byron was kind, easy-going, professional, and as she got to know him she realized he was also very attractive. True, he was no Brad Pitt, or Tom Brady, but he was very attractive in his own right. The more she thought about it, the more she decided that maybe the time was right to move things along.

"Well, it looks like we're here." Beginning a sentence with "well" was a clear sign that Byron too hoped to move things along.

"I guess it's your turn," Julie said. "Do you have an upcoming activity where you need a wife present?"

Julie was sure he would have a long list. After all, if he wanted to see her twice a month he must have had all sorts of things he was constantly making excuses for. So she was surprised to see that his first response was, "Well . . . I . . . um."

"Didn't you say your assistant was always looking for a double date?"

"She was, but she's on like a full month honeymoon. I guess that's one of the perks to marrying later in life when you both have a little extra cash," Byron said

"Well okay, just let me know when something comes up." She began to step out of the car.

"Well, actually, Julie, I."

Julie could sense he was nervous.

"I was wondering if you just wanted to catch dinner and a movie."

Dinner and a movie, the ultimate "I didn't plan anything, not sure what to do date" But in this rare instance, Byron had struck the right note. It made it overwhelmingly clear that he had nothing going on, no commitment to have his bride with him, rather he was asking to be with her because he wanted to spend time with her.

"That would be wonderful," Julie responded.

Byron was now the one ready to be elated. "Great, then I'll pick you up Saturday at 5:00 p.m. two weeks from today," he said as he got out of the car and headed to her door.

Julie was a little disappointed that the two weeks hadn't turned into one but she figured, one step at a time, as Byron opened her door. Julie got out, Byron closed the door and now the two just stood. They still had no real established way of saying goodbye and neither really felt it was their place to make the move. Byron had far more experience with suppressing his hormones than he had in letting them dictate his actions and, at thirty-five, their power to dictate was not what it once was. Julie could see that he was going to be a perfect gentleman and while the side hug might become a face-to-face hug, she couldn't expect much more. But if movies had taught her anything, it was that even the most perfect gentleman outside can be something very different when invited beyond the threshold. "Do you want to come in for a minute?"

"Sure, that would be great," Byron said as they headed in.

Once inside they sat next to each other on the couch and continued their conversation. The problem in Julie's mind was: that was all they did. Whatever magic thresholds had on every actor in every movie she could see was not working on Byron. He was as much a gentleman inside as he had been outside. Julie wasn't sure what he was waiting for. She could have understood if he wanted to claim high morals but that didn't work because they were married.

In the end, she did get that hug. It was nice, just like the conversation was but Julie couldn't help but wonder, *What's wrong with this guy, or what's wrong with me?*

This date began a wonderful, yet incredibly frustrating, pattern for Julie. Once a month she would plan a fun, often group date, and once a month they went to get dinner and a movie. The more they dated, the closer friends they became, and the closer friends they became, the more Julie despised that word.

Byron was as anxious for things to move along as Julie. He kept saying, *next time I'll kiss her,* or *next time I'll tell her I love her.* The only thing common in all his ideas was, next time. And that is how it remained, next time, and they both came to accept that perhaps things could work out, even if they were married and "just friends."

Chapter 19

Smooth Charlie

"Julie, I have that architect on the phone again," came the voice on the speaker phone.

"How many times is this guy going to call? Go ahead and put him through." She took a deep breath and then smiled and tried to sound polite. "Hi James, you call to tell me you finally agreed that the design you submitted will collapse the very first time there is two inches of snow?"

"Very funny. I actually called to warn you."

"Warn me?"

"The guy whose cabin we have been working on is on his way over."

"On his way over?"

"I told him what you told me, that we would need to add that support in the front room, and he said he wanted to talk to you. I told him we could call you but when he saw how close your office was, he decided to head over there. My guess is he will be there any," a beep took out his last word indicating another call, it was the front desk.

"Thanks for the warning," Julie said before switching to the other call, "Send him up."

"Oh, were you expecting him? Good thing because he's on his way."

A few moments later a man was standing in her doorway. As far as attractiveness goes, this man was found lacking. What he lacked was a warning that should have followed him, warning all females that they were about to discover that George Clooney didn't look as good as they thought. No, this man had it all, over six feet tall, dark, thick wavy hair, a gruff shadow that was no beard, but well past five o'clock, and a build that a Greek god would have been jealous of. Was he perfect? Of course not. Julie knew that perfection did not exist and this man was no exception, for a quick glance revealed a rather odd looking mole on his forehead.

"Hello, sir. Can I help you?" Julie said as she stood.

The stranger waved his hand near his face, catching in midair the mole as it flew away from his now perfect face. "Julie? Um . . . I'm Charles Nordstrom. You are working on my cabin."

"Yes, I am familiar with the project."

Surprise filled Charles's face. "Um . . . I . . . ah . . . wanted to talk to you about it."

"Yes, go ahead."

"I guess I didn't expect you to be, well I expected something else."

"What do you mean?"

"Well, first of all, your names on the plans are J. Smith, P.E. and, well, you aren't what I expected a professional engineer to well . . . "

"I see, you didn't know I was a woman."

"Yes, but that's not the biggest thing. You're supposed to have glasses and a pocket protector, maybe slightly overweight."

"Am I?" Julie responded. "So, now that you see me as my true self, do you still want to talk, or do you need me to go put on a pocket protector before we begin?"

"I guess we can talk, but I'm finding it much harder to say what I had planned."

"Why is that?" Julie was loving this. She loved being a woman in a man's field especially when she was able to catch them in their surprise.

"I guess it's just that I planned to have it out with you, and I think it would have been easier if you were, well, how I envisioned you, and not as you are. It's hard to have it out with an attractive woman."

Blushing a bit, she responded, "You will find me very capable of holding my own. Let me have it."

"Ok, you asked for it. Here I go. That support you want right in my main room is uglier than the person I pictured you to be."

"If that was your prepared speech, you might want to spend more time at the drafting board."

"Forget the speech, what about the support? You are an engineer, figure out how to hold up my house with just the main beam, can't you just make it bigger or something."

"Yes, it would need to be about twice as deep . . . and steel. Which may take away from your mountain rustic look."

"Well then, we need to come up with something else. I don't want a support in the main room."

"I thought of several other options, but your architect wasn't interested."

"I'm all ears."

"If we moved this wall in," she said, pulling out a set of plans, "you could expand the other portion of the room. It would open up the kitchen and give you just as much space overall. I think it would also improve your view out the main window, but I haven't been up there to check."

"We can change that. It's about an hour away, let's go."

"Now?"

"Sure. I don't want my engineer making decisions about what my view will be if she doesn't even know what the views are," Charles said.

"I do like to see the proposed sites, but you'd be amazed how often it's not in the budget."

"It's my project and it's in my budget."

"Well, okay. I think I can shuffle a few things. Let's do it."

And before she knew it, she was sitting next to Charles on her way to Mt. Charleston. Julie had never been one for fancy cars, she liked practical vehicles. But she had to admit there was a bit of a rush as she slid into the perfectly formed shotgun seat of Charles's Porsche 911.

"So how does a gorgeous girl like you end up signing their name with the letters P.E. after it?"

"I was good at math and engineering, just made sense."

"I noticed a ring, what does your husband do? Is he a nurse or a school teacher?" Yes, much of what Charles said was borderline sexist, or maybe way across the border, but something about how he said it made it not bother her. She had always been opposed to people getting away with things just because of their looks, but . . . he looked so good.

"No, turns out my husband is a marriage counselor."

"Wow. That has to be the worst."

"Why?"

"Is he always analyzing everything you do? Or does he ever ask you how you feel?"

This question actually stung Julie more than she expected. She knew what he meant, after all, if he did always ask her how she felt it would be really annoying. But while she didn't doubt that Byron did ask his clients how they felt, he had never, ever asked her how she felt. And despite liking Byron a lot, she had never really expressed deeper feelings to him. The question reminded her that, in part, it was because he never asked. She did not want to look like an unstable individual, but as the thoughts ran through her head, she was literally holding back her emotions as she said, "No, he doesn't."

"I'm sorry, I didn't mean to bring up anything I shouldn't."

"No, it's fine. I guess, like all relationships, mine and my husband's is complicated."

"Well, I know you can handle complicated, at least I hope you can, because I want the most beautiful cabin on Mt. Charleston, no matter how complicated the design has to be."

This was a perfect chance to get the focus back onto work and they continued discussing the cabin until they pulled up into a vacant lot that sat on top of a beautiful vista in Mt. Charleston. After months of only seeing buildings, dirt, and a few cactus plants, the view Julie now got to enjoy was amazing. The temperature was a perfect chilly 65 degrees, much nicer than the 104 degrees they had left down in the valley. Pines reached up to a clear blue sky in every direction, except for a small clearing of meadow with wild grass and wildflowers that sat directly in front of the patch that had been cleared for the cabin. Across the small valley carved by the stream that ran through the canyon was a jagged snowcapped peak. "I don't get up here nearly enough," whispered Julie to herself as she took a deep breath of cold air.

"Me neither." Charles came from behind her. "But you are going to solve that by getting my cabin back on track. So, let's figure out if you can get me the best view possible and avoid any pillars in my living space." They pulled out the plans and began to place rocks and branches how the cabin was to be laid out.

"See, we turn this wall slightly and bring it in about three feet. Then we can move this wall out a little, giving you a larger dining space, and your view will be perfectly aligned to see a bighorn sheep crest over that mountain just as the sun sets behind the peak in the evening."

"You have me convinced. Let's do it," Charles said.

"I thought it might work out for the best," Julie said as she rubbed her arms.

"Here, I have a jacket in the car," Charles said as he opened his car and pulled out a leather jacket. He draped the much too large jacket over Julie's shoulders.

"Well, now that we have the issue solved. Maybe we better get heading back," Julie said.

"Seems like a waste to get all the way up here and only spend our time talking about work. Shouldn't we enjoy ourselves for a minute. Here, pull up a chair in my living room and enjoy the view," Charles said, as he grabbed two stumps that were left behind from some of the trees that had been cleared for his cabin lot. He turned them over and gestured to Julie to sit down.

"I guess I can stay for a few minutes."

"Plus, I want to see if that Bighorn sheep is going to crest over the peak at sunset like you claim," Charles added.

"Sunset won't be for a few hours."

"Are you saying this view you're trying to convince me is so great, isn't worth a few hours?"

"I can stay for a little while, but not much more."

"Okay, I'll take it. So, how long have you been married to Mr. Complicated?"

"Why are we talking about my marriage?" Julie asked.

"We need to talk about something while we wait for that goat to show up."

"It's a sheep, and why don't you tell me about you? Are you married, any kids?"

"It's complicated."

"That's cheating, you can't avoid the issue by using my excuse," Julie said. She worried he was becoming too casual with a client but something about Charles made being this casual seem very natural.

"Well, if you want to know. No kids and I am currently in the market as it were," Charles said.

"Oh yes, the wonderful market. How is it?"

"Much like Netflix, millions of options and none that seem worthwhile. You're lucky to be married."

"I guess, in some ways."

"No really, do you know how hard it is to find a decent member of the opposite sex. One who has a stable life, hasn't been married three times before or isn't some kind of basket case?" Charles's passion on the subject was clear. "Not only that, I am constantly being set up only to find out on the back end that the person makes Medusa seem sane."

"I completely understand," Julie could sympathize with all sincerity.

"You probably don't even remember what it was like."

"I have only been married for three years, and before my marriage I felt exactly like you did."

"So, how did you find Mr. Right? I suppose you didn't meet him at his work."

"You're right there. But if I had, that would have been quite a story." She stopped there and Charles looked down as if to say, go on. She took a deep breath and said, "Um . . . we met through an ad in the paper."

"An ad in the paper?" Charles questioned.

"I don't know why I told you that. It's weird and the whole situation is weird. I think we better talk about something else."

"You can't leave the story like that. You have to tell me now. Come on, what is said on the mountain stays on the mountain."

"Oh fine, but don't tell anyone. I can't even believe I'm telling you. But the quick version is that my husband is a marriage counselor who needed a wife for credibility, so he put an ad in the paper and I responded and we got married."

"What? That's a joke right?" he said as he looked over at Julie. "Oh, you're serious. Wow. I guess . . . you were right, that is complicated. You just replied to that ad? Wasn't that kind of scary."

"Yes, I wasn't at a very good spot at the time, and like you said, it's hard to find anyone worthwhile out there, so I replied. Luckily, Byron was a sensible man."

"I have to agree with that. Also, very practical. Need wife, get wife."

"Don't make fun of him. He's a good guy."

"That's quite the 'how you met' story. So, has it worked out?"

Julie wanted to say, "Yes, Byron's great. It's worked out fine." But she couldn't. The thought of her what she now coined 'loveless marriage' with its never-ending two week dates and lack of any physical affection had worn on her. She longed for something more so, as much as she wanted to say it had worked out, all she could do was with a small tear say, "Sometimes I'm not so sure I made the right choice."

Charles, unlike Byron, knew exactly when the scene called for physical affection. He reached a long, muscular arm around Julie as she leaned into his chest. She could hardly believe it. She was a married woman with a client on a construction site, cuddling. It was so wrong, but it felt so good. She sat in his warm arms leaning against his chest for a moment, but then she thought of Byron. Not only was she married, she was married to a good and decent man. He may not be affectionate, but he still always treated her with kindness and respect and at least enjoyed dating her. No, as good as this felt, it had to stop, "Charles, I really need to go," she said as she stood up.

"Oh, okay. I guess that poor sheep will have to do his mountain cresting act without an audience. Shall we?" He walked toward the car and opened the passenger door.

Charles quickly moved back to lighter topics on the way home. He was a fun conversationalist and any awkwardness from the afternoon soon left. Julie enjoyed the conversation until they got closer to the office. "It's getting late, I'd be happy to get you some dinner."

"No, I better go home."

"Well, if you change your mind, or just need to talk, here's my number," he said as he walked her to her car.

"Thanks Charles, but I really need to go home."

"Okay, but don't hesitate to call. I mean it," he said as he walked back to his car with a smile.

She tried to take deep breaths as she saw him drive away. She sat paralyzed behind the steering wheel. Confusion filled her mind. On one hand, Byron was a good man. She kept repeating that. She enjoyed his company, and he seemed to enjoy hers. And they had committed to each other. Even if it was weird, it was a commitment. On the other hand, she so wanted to feel loved, to hold someone, to be held, the way she felt tonight in Charles's arms. His phone number was staring back at her. If she would dial, in a few minutes a gorgeous man in a Porsche would come back into view and she could once again be in his arms. She knew she shouldn't, but she didn't want to lose the option either.

He is a client, so I better save his number, she rationalized as she put his contact information into her phone. Once in the phone, she again resumed the staring contest but now with the phone and it's newly held contact information. All of the sudden, "Dad" came across the screen.

"Hey, Dad," Julie said after swiping her finger across the phone.

"Hey, Jules. How are you?"

"Just leaving work. What's up?"

"Well, it turns out your mother and I are going to be back in Vegas in two weeks and we wondered if we could stay with you and Byron."

"Oh, sure. That shouldn't be an issue."

"Is Byron going to be in town?"

"Sure, I think so. I can check when I see him, but I assume he will be."

"You two, doing good?"

"Yeah, we're doing fine."

"Would you say things have been getting better?" Julie was beginning to wonder what was going on. Her mom had always been interested in her relationship with Byron, but her dad rarely showed interest.

"I guess so, but I never thought things were bad. Did Byron tell you they were, when you two talked?"

"Oh no, he just mentioned to me you two were dating more and it's always amazing how much dating helps."

"What do you mean, Dad?"

"Oh, nothing. Byron and I mentioned dating and I told him how I always made sure to take your mom on a date a couple times a month and it made a big difference in our relationship."

"A couple times a month? So, like, every other week?"

"Yes, that is what your mom and I do, or did, we probably aren't as good about it as we used to be."

Suddenly it was all becoming clear to Julie. It wasn't because Byron wanted to see her at all. "Dad, did you make Byron take me on dates every other week?"

"No." He paused. "I wouldn't say 'make.'"

Julie couldn't believe it. It was just another business deal. "Dad. You had no right. My relationships are my business. Stay out of it."

She heard her dad begin to say, "Now Julie—," but she wasn't going to stick around for the rest. Hanging up, she looked down at her phone. Charles's contact information was still up, and she knew exactly what to do.

"Charles? You still hungry?"

Chapter 20

The Kiss

Byron knew, when it came to dating, he was as spineless as a jellyfish, and not a particularly gutsy one either. For almost a year now he had been faithfully following his father-in-laws prescription of two dates a month, but despite this he had seen third grade couples at recess get further along physically than he had achieved with his wife. Both verbally, and physically he had failed to show Julie any of his bottled-up feelings, but Thursday would be different.

Saturday was their typical date night, but Thursday, and a week earlier than needed, he was going to ask her out. Why Thursday? Because Thursday was their third anniversary. Debating what to do and how to do it had been bouncing around in his head for weeks and it was now clear what he was going to do.

Byron knew himself. He was not the sly devil who could tell a fishing story that got his arms going wider and wider until they were finally around Julie. No, if he could handle subtle attraction and moving in, he would not be in the predicament he was in. It had to be a clear statement of how he felt and then hope that she would accept it and throw herself into his arms.

The plan was simple, take Julie to a fancy restaurant. At first, he had thought about going back to the small sandwich shop where they had first met. After all, that is where they had their first good conversation and where they had decided they would get married. But the problem was that it was more a casual lunch shop than a fancy dinner one. In the end, he settled on taking her across the street to the Eiffel tower. It was the perfect atmosphere and it had played a role, albeit an awkward one, on their first date. The jewelry shop where they had purchased her wedding ring was still in business and so he had them make a custom necklace and earrings both with tear drop diamonds that matched her wedding ring.

With the necklace and earrings in hand, he was now again staring at Julie's contact information. His mind raced over all the times he had sat staring at his phone with the plan to call her. There was their wedding night when he never dared to make the call, and there was two years later when he was worried about asking her out and it ended up being her bank, and all the times in between. Regularly asking her out for a year should have made him less fearful, but somehow this was different. Not only was it a Thursday on an off week, but this was it, the big moment. Either she would throw herself into his arms and they would finally be really married or she would say, "Byron, that wasn't the arrangement. Have you been playing me this whole time, pretending you only needed a fake wife but deep down you wanted a real one?" He decided he better go for a run to clear his head. Then he would call her.

"I'm glad you called. What made you change your mind?" Charles said as Julie hopped back into his Porsche.

"I had a phone call that made it clear that I need to live my own life."

"Wow. Sounds like an important call," Charles said.

"I think it was." Vocalizing it made it sink in all that much more.

"Well, I can't wait to hear about it. Sushi?"

"You bet."

To her it was a sign. The one food Byron had always refused to get was sushi. She loved it; he hated it. Julie was so full of emotions she had to talk to someone about what was going on in her head, and talk she did. She told Charles everything about the phone call. She even included her frustration with her "loveless" marriage, and how she now saw clearly that Byron was only seeing her out of duty, not love.

"So, Byron has been going on dates with you because your dad told him to?" Charles confirmed after hearing her tell of her phone call.

"I think that pretty much sums it up," Julie said.

"What a wimp," Charles shot back.

"My dad is the one to blame. He shouldn't have gotten involved. Byron was just doing what he thought was right."

"Oh, I don't mean he is a wimp for doing what your dad asked. If any man tells me to date his attractive daughter, I would do it. I think he's a wimp for going on all these dates and never doing anything."

"What do you mean?"

"You said you two never even kissed."

"I think on the cheek, on our wedding day."

"Like I said . . . wimp."

Julie didn't like the negativity about Byron. She was a little upset with him for not telling her about her dad forcing the dates, but felt, beyond that, he was not at fault. "He can't help if he isn't attracted to me."

"Okay, he's not a wimp. He's blind."

She smiled. She didn't mind this talk anymore. "Let's not talk about Byron. Tell me about yourself."

This was something Charles was a master at and quickly the night rolled into very thrilling stories of Charles's heroic life. He'd been all over the world—Indonesia, Ukraine, Thailand, and more. And his activities were as exotic as the locations—heli-skiing, rock climbing, kayaking, scuba diving, and some sort of sport with natives that sounded like half the team died. Each story, while unique, all had the same punch line, "And that's when I jumped in and cut the vine just in time to save Bill from what would have been a very unseemly death." Charles clearly didn't call it a day's work if he hadn't yanked some poor sap's head out of an unsuspecting tiger's jaw.

Julie was amazed that this guy would give her the time of day, and she began to very much regret that the only thing that seemed to stand in the way of her being on the next trip to Antarctica barely missing sudden death from a herd of stampeding penguins and being swept up by Charles's large muscular arms that he kept conveniently by his side, was her, now very inconvenient, marriage to Byron.

As the night wore on, the more inconvenient the marriage became, and the more she wished she could just forget Byron existed. But she couldn't. The more she enjoyed it, the more guilty she felt. Yes, her dad should have stayed out of her private life but that didn't change the fact that she was married to Byron. One can debate if it's okay for a married woman to have dinner with a client, but she knew this was much, much more than just a dinner with a client. She was having emotions and thoughts no married woman, no matter how weird the relationship, should have about another man.

After Charles paid the tab and they began to walk out to his car, she worried how far she would let this go. She didn't want to do anything she would regret but was secretly worried that the part of her that didn't want it to stop would win. That was when she remembered with some relief and some regret that he was not dropping her off at home, but back at her work parking lot where they had left her car. A few minutes later and they were there.

"I'm really glad you changed your mind and decided to come to dinner. I really enjoyed it," Charles said.

"I did too," Julie admitted. Before she could get out, he had turned off the car and run around to get her door. "Thanks."

"No problem," he said and she saw that he was following her as she walked towards her car. She got out her keys and pushed the unlock, shaking badly enough that she actually pushed it two or three times as the car beeped.

Once at the door, she turned and Charles was right there, staring into her eyes. Why did he have to be so good at this? If he had politely asked if they could kiss, she might have gotten up the courage to say no, but as he got closer, she knew the only way now was to turn away or cry out, "stop." Neither of which she had the courage, or the desire, to do.

Guilt and excitement blended in an odd cocktail of emotions that rushed over her as she leaned in for a kiss. This was no peck. Charles's arms enveloped her body as they pressed together as warmly and tightly as their lips. She instinctively put her arms around him and let herself enjoy the feelings she had so longed to feel. It felt so good . . . until she saw Byron's face. Somewhere while the kiss continued she suddenly could only see Byron in her mind. With guilt overtaking excitement, she pulled her arms from around him and lightly pushed away as she pulled her lips back. "Charles, I had a great time, but I really need to go."

"Oh, no problem. So, when do I get to take you back to the site and discuss the cabin again?"

"I don't know if we really need to go on-site again."

"Well, just in case, how about we go back to the cabin after dinner on Saturday?"

"I um . . . yeah that will work."

"See you then, Julie."

She got into her car and watched him pull away. She sat for a moment and then began to cry. She didn't know if it was tears of sorrow or joy, but for either reason the tears flowed, until . . . the phone rang.

She pulled up the phone and cleared her tears to see who it was. It was Byron.

Chapter 21

The Talk

She did her best to collect herself and answered. "Hello Byron."
"Hi, Julie. Are you okay?"

"Yeah, I'm fine."

"Are you sure? If you like, I could call back, or maybe there's something I can do?"

Sure, now he gets this way. "No, I'm fine. I'm just watching a romance."

"Which one? Is it any good?"

"It's a Hallmark, you know, typical girl surrounded by good looking men and can't decide between the rich doctor or the rich lawyer."

"She should find a good marriage counselor and choose him." As Byron laughed at his own joke, Julie hit the mute button so she could cry. "Well, I was calling because I wanted to see if you would be willing to go with me to dinner tomorrow."

"Tomorrow?" The timing surprised her. Instantly she began to wonder if her dad was behind this.

"I know it's not Saturday or my week but I have something I want to talk to you about."

"What?" she said, trying to mask her suspicion.

"I'd rather wait. If tomorrow doesn't work, we could do another night."

"No, tomorrow works."

"Great. I have reservations at the Eiffel tower downtown at The Paris for six. So, I'll pick you up around 5:30?"

Julie wasn't sure what was happening but given some of what was going on, she decided some options might be good, and as she learned tonight having her own vehicle gave her those. "Byron, can I just meet you there?"

"Oh . . . yeah . . . sure," Byron said.

"Thanks, see you then."

She hung up but definitely wasn't done talking. For the last six months Byron had become her closest confidant and tonight Charles had stepped into that role, but neither of those seemed like the right choice. So, she dialed up her old friend Becky.

"Hey Jules, to what do I owe the pleasure?" Becky asked.

"We need to talk. Can you come over?"

"Do you want something to drink?" Julie asked as her friend came into the house.

"No, I'm fine. Let's sit down and get to business, this is serious. You haven't had me over to your place in ages and then you call me up on a weeknight, saying you need to talk. Girl, I knew big news was coming, so lay it on me. Is Byron home?"

"No, he kind of doesn't live here," Julie admitted.

"Doesn't live here? So that's why we always meet at restaurants or my house. Okay, What is going on, girl?"

"I haven't been exactly honest about Byron?"

"You two fightin'?"

"No," Julie said, more defensive than she meant to be.

"Oh, okay, so he's seeing another woman?"

"No."

"He actually lives in a different town with his real wife?"

"No."

"You two are divorced?"

Becky rattled this off as fast as Julie could cough out the negative monosyllables, and she finally decided this guessing had to stop. "We were never really married."

Becky determined that they didn't call it a throw pillow for nothing and put it to good use hitting Julie harmlessly on her shoulder. "What do you mean? I was at your wedding. I saw a priestly man say, 'I pronounce you husband and wife.' Well, he almost said it, before Byron yacked . . . It was all a show? Byron did some fake yacking to stop it from being official?"

"That is not . . . "

"Because that is some clever trickery. You two are sly ones," Becky interrupted.

"The throw-up was real."

"It was very convincing, the smell and all. So, he took a pill to make him vomit, just at the right time and . . . "

"No, that part wasn't planned. I mean, the wedding was, not the vomiting, but it was a real wedding." Julie tried to think how to explain, "But we've never really been married."

"You girl, do not make sense . . . wait, you mean you never, um . . . how do you say, duh, nun a nah."

"What?" Julie asked.

"You know, consolidated the marriage."

"You mean consummated?"

"You know what I mean."

"Not just that," Julie said.

"What do you mean, not just that. That is a lot of just. Is Byron gay?"

"No. I don't think so. I mean I've never really asked him. But we're getting off point."

"Jules, whether or not your husband is gay, is likely very on point, and you might want to ask if you are wondering why he's not affectionate."

"Okay, we are definitely off point." Julie took a deep breath trying to figure out how she could get a little more clarity in the conversation. "You remember a little while before the wedding you set me up with Ricky."

"Yes?" Becky said as she tapped the side of her chin with her finger. "I was always surprised you two didn't go out again. I thought you had a great time, and whenever I tried to call and ask you what happened, you got all weird. Next thing I know you were marrying some marriage counselor."

"Becky, the truth is, I had a great time with Ricky. He said he wasn't ready to move on from his wife."

"Hey, that reminds me," Becky jumped in. "Ricky got remarried last month."

"Not helping," Julie said.

"Sorry. Go on."

"I was devastated. And really frustrated with dating and set ups. That's when I remembered the ad you showed me earlier that day."

"Wait . . . Byron is the ad guy?" Becky asked.

Julie quietly nodded.

"I can't believe it. You actually responded to that ad, and married him!"

Julie's head continued its steady up and down motion.

"That is nuts, I can't believe it. And you didn't tell me!"

"I know, I should have," Julie acknowledged.

"So, that's why Byron is never around."

"Yeah, so anyways . . . "

"No, no, no 'so anyways.' I need to process this. You married a total stranger, just to avoid dating."

"Can we move on?" Julie asked.

"I still can't believe you married Ad Man. And . . . " Clearly a sudden realization struck Becky. "You owe me money!"

"And how is that?"

"I remember when I brought you that ad. I told you I got a 25 percent finder's fee."

"You were joking. And it was not twenty-five percent."

"Okay twenty percent, either way, you owe me."

"Well, I could pay you." Julie hadn't thought about the money for a long time. "I haven't touched a penny of it."

"What?"

"I felt too weird. So it just sits there."

"Okay, my fee is one-hundred percent. I won't feel weird." It was Becky's turn to take a breath. "Now you can move on."

"Thank you," Julie said sarcastically as she finally got to the whole reason she had called Becky over. "See the problem is, I think I need a divorce."

"Julie, you are married to a man who's only involvement with you is putting money in the bank. Money, I might add, that can flow to me. You have the perfect husband, why get a divorce?"

"Well, for one thing, that is not his only involvement."

"Oh, you've been seeing your husband. Is that why we finally got to meet him at the book club?" Becky asked.

"Yes."

"Do you hate spending time with him? You two seemed to get along fine."

"Yeah, our dates are fine, and he is all right to talk to." Julie looked over at Becky as she again searched for the right words. "But that is all we ever do, talk."

"Oh yeah, back to the gay thing."

"Can you forget about the gay thing? I think I know why there is only talk. He's not interested, and don't you dare say because he's gay."

"Then why would he keep seeing you?" Becky asked.

"I found out tonight that my dad has been making him."

"Like a gun to his head. Take my daughter out . . . or else."

"No, I don't know how he made him. My dad is very persuasive," Julie said.

"I don't know girl, if a guy keeps seeing you, my guess is he at least likes being with you, or else he would just send the checks. I still can't believe you found a guy who sends you checks every month. So, my advice. If you like talking to him, and are willing to give me the money, just enjoy this thing and don't worry about your dad. You two are old enough to decide to play marriage if you want to."

"Well, there is one more thing." Julie gave an awkward smile. "There is this guy."

"Whoa. Hold up. Are you cheating on your pretend husband?"

"No! Well . . . um . . . I'm not cheating . . . per se."

Becky reached for another appropriately named pillow, but Julie was too quick and her arms were up ready to block any projectiles. Becky huffed, put the pillow back on the couch, and said, "You better get me something to drink or at least let me lie down for this next part."

"Don't get dramatic. I just need some advice," Julie said.

"Don't get dramatic!" Becky took a breath. "I find out my best friend has had a sham marriage for years, has been shafting me out of my agent fee, and now find out she's cheating on her sham husband. All without my knowledge. And I'm not supposed to be dramatic. I think we all know who is the one putting on a drama here."

"Okay, so it's a bit complicated," Julie admitted.

"So, as I hyperventilate, tell me again, who is this guy?"

"He's a client, who . . . "

"A client? In your engineering job, right?"

"And what other job would it be?" Julie was not fond of the question.

"I don't know. You're coming clean on a lot tonight."

"Charles Nordstrom is a . . . "

"Does he own the store?"

"I don't know what he does, but he is a client who I'm working with designing his cabin, and we went to dinner tonight to discuss work, but we ended up discussing . . . other things too."

"I see, dinner with Smooth Charlie to discuss 'work'," Becky said.

"Don't use air quotes with me." Julie may be the one who needed to apologize for holding back information for a few years, but even in her apologetic state she had limits. "Anyway, tonight he kissed me."

"Wow. This is serious. Does this Smooth Charlie know you're married?" Becky asked.

"He knows the situation. And can we call him, just Charles."

"And I guess you liked this kiss?"

"Yeah. I did. It felt really good, except for the guilt that I felt when I realized I'm a married woman kissing another man."

"So, you really like this Smooth . . . I mean this just Charles," Becky said.

"I don't know if I like him, but I liked finally touching, kissing, being loved and wanted, and wanting and loving in return. I'm not sure I will ever have that in my current marriage."

Becky began to speak but Julie cut her off. "Please, don't say anything bad about Byron. We like each other and I think that is all. And

I think I want the freedom to pursue something more, to pursue love, with someone, maybe Charles."

The two women who had immense love and respect for each other looked into each other's eyes. Julie knew exactly why she'd called her best friend to finally get out what had been in her heart. Becky wiped a tear from her eye. "I guess now is when I give you my amazing advice. I'd charge you for it, but you already owe me so much, why bother. My advice is simple. You need to talk to Byron."

The greeter knew he recognized the man as he approached. Of course, being a greeter at a popular restaurant like the Eiffel Tower on the strip of Las Vegas did lend itself to seeing a lot of people, but there was something special about this face that now approached him. He couldn't quite place it and continued to rack his brain as he came close enough for contact.

"May I help you?"

"I have a table, under Lewis."

"Yes, we have your table. Would you prefer to wait here or at the table?"

"I better wait here for my wife. Oh, here she comes now," Byron said as Julie approached. As soon as Julie's face came into view, the greeter realized who was in front of him. He had told hundreds if not thousands of the night, three years ago, when a man had come in the restaurant with a woman, met yet a different woman, all three bearing a red rose. The clear rejection of girl number two was in and of itself something to remember. Looking again at Byron he recalled the last thing he had ever spoken to this man about—it was leaving him with his credit card information and a commitment to pay whatever bill the women left behind. The woman was clearly miserable, but with the gentleman's commitment came the opportunity for her to share her pain. That wine bill was legendary and the only thing that eclipsed it was the tip she left at the bottom of his credit card receipt.

For weeks they expected to hear that the man, long gone before the full extent of the damage was realized, would contest the near thousand-dollar bill. But such tidings would never come, and the greeter assumed that the man, Byron Lewis, according to this reservation had been true to his word to cover the cost. He was excited to see Byron again, but was quite dismayed when he asked, "Are you expecting anyone else?" and Byron replied, "No."

Clearly it appeared that tonight would be much less legendary, thought the greeter as he sat the couple in the same table they had been at three years before.

"Do you remember this place?" Byron asked.

"How could I forget? You didn't bring me here to meet another Julie, did you?"

"I sure hope not. Sometimes I still worry that I'll run into her in a grocery store and she will try to force me to marry her. Thank goodness, if it ever happens, I'm not single."

Byron had hoped for a laugh, but all he got was Julie avoiding eye contact and squirming slightly in her seat. What was wrong? He could never think of a time things had been so awkward between them.

They sat quietly and Byron reached into his pocket to feel the necklace case. He debated if now was the right time, or should he wait until after the food had shown up, or maybe until after they ate? A bit more small talk was probably appropriate but being focused on his mission made it hard to come up with anything to say.

Byron knew why he was nervous. What he couldn't figure out was, why was Julie? She looked as uneasy as he was. *Why would that be?* he thought. She wasn't about to bare her heart today. Actually, he hoped that she would, but not until after he did. This was all hard enough as it was. Julie acting this way was really making it harder.

Usually, the two spoke openly and freely, but today was different and it was a long pause before Byron finally said, "Last time we were here, things were very different. I know I felt very differently."

"How's that?" Julie asked, in a much less encouraging fashion than Byron had hoped.

"Well for one, we had just met. But I feel that I know you so much better now. Do you realize what today is?" Byron asked.

"Thursday?"

Byron had many women in his office complain about men not remembering their anniversary and always thought they were a bit melodramatic for such a small thing. He realized he would never feel that way again. "It's our third wedding anniversary."

Julie looked shocked and a little guilty. "It was good of you to remember. This is the first anniversary I've ever celebrated with someone. I guess I didn't allow myself to look forward to them," Julie admitted.

"That makes sense, and I apologize for that," Byron said.

"For what? That's what I signed up for, right?"

"Ever wonder if there is more? More than what we currently have?"

Had she ever! Why was he saying this? Had he found another woman and discovered, like she had with Charles, that there was more. Her mind told her that if that was the case, she should be happy for him. After all, she was just about to dump him, but her heart told her something very different.

"Julie, what I want to say is." He reached into his pocket and was beginning to withdraw the case when—

"Can I get you two anything to drink?" Byron hadn't even noticed the waiter approaching.

"Oh, Julie do you want anything?"

"Water is fine."

"Me too. Water is good."

The waiter walked off, along with Byron's thought process.

"You were saying?" Julie asked.

Byron thought he better work his way back into it.

"I was wondering if you wanted a chance to have something more. I mean, I see how happy your parents are and . . . "

"Why would you bring them up?" Julie was beginning to see what was going on. She now realized that the only reason he was taking her out on their anniversary was because her dad told him to.

"I thought they seemed like a good couple."

"Byron, did you start taking me on dates because my dad asked you to?"

Byron had not expected that question and stared at her, not knowing what to say. But he could tell that his silence was already saying too much and decided to come clean. "He encouraged me to."

"And so you have only been seeing me because my dad asked you to?"

"No, I've really enjoyed seeing you," he said, trying to recover the situation.

"We go out every two weeks, like clockwork. How often did my dad ask you to take me out?"

"Um . . ." Byron took a sip of water. "He did think that twice a month would be a good idea."

"I see."

"Julie, I want you to know that . . ." His mind was saying the words of "I love you and I want us to be together" but he couldn't quite get it out. " . . . that I really liked the time we had together."

"Had?"

"I didn't mean that. I meant . . ."

"Byron. I need to tell you something."

"Yes?"

Julie took a deep breath. "Byron, I met someone."

Byron was shocked. People meet people every day but he could tell that this someone was more. "Who did you meet?"

"His name is Charles."

"Oh, I guess, I didn't . . ." He didn't know what to say. He wanted to say that meeting people was not part of the rules, but knew that trying to stop love was something that was difficult to do.

"Byron, I didn't mean for this to happen. It was just a guy I was doing work for, and we were meeting for work and it has turned into something more. I wasn't trying to break up our marriage, but I feel something, I feel like he wants to be with me."

As Julie spoke, the world began to spin. Byron had a hard time focusing as the scene in front of him grew blurry. She continued on and he tried to concentrate but knew he was becoming more and more despondent.

"Byron, you said it yourself, I want more, more than we have had. I want to be really and truly loved. I think I have a chance. I think I need to take that chance. Don't you feel that we need more, that we could have more? If you had a chance at that, wouldn't you give anything to take it?"

Byron could see exactly what she meant and agreed completely. He wanted to say, "Yes, that is exactly right, we need more and we can have more together. I want us to discover 'the more' together," but all he could get out was, "Yes, I understand."

"So, I'm sorry, Byron, but I would like a divorce."

His world stopped. He knew he had no one to blame but himself, and could see no way to stop this reasonable path forward. He was too late. He was trying not to, but tears began to come down his face.

"Byron, I never wanted to hurt you and you don't deserve this but," she paused as she wiped a small tear, "you understand, right?"

"I understand."

"I will give you all the money back," Julie said.

"No, you keep the money." Byron couldn't focus, the room was spinning. He tried to continue the conversation but couldn't think of anything. He wanted to be alone, for the world to close in around him. After a painful pause he finally got out, "I hope things work out with Charles."

"Thanks." She didn't know what to do. They hadn't ordered and the rest of the night was bound to be nothing but awkward. "Byron, I think I better go." As she spoke, her phone rang and she looked down.

Byron was trying to gather himself. "Who is that?"

Somewhat embarrassed, she said, "It's Charles. I better go."

She stood up and so did Byron. She looked through her moist eyes at his that were even more so. They leaned in and hugged, "Byron, it really was a good marriage. Thanks for everything."

"No, thank you. I will always remember you."

"Me too."

She walked out as he whispered below the hum of happier conversations, "I love you, and always will."

Chapter 22

The Discovery

The lake was exactly the way Byron remembered it. Five a.m. was early for Byron. He couldn't recall the last time he'd been up this early, definitely not in the past decade. He had stared at his alarm clock, daring it to continue its blaring, hoping that it was incorrect about the time and that he could return to sleep. But now that he saw the fog slowly clearing as he and his father sat quietly in his father's small rowboat, casting out into the perfectly placid water, he was grateful to be up.

The sun crested over the horizon as Byron realized it had been far too long since he had found himself so busily doing nothing. After Julie had asked for a divorce, he quickly cleared his calendar and decided to get away. He didn't care where, just away. Without knowing where else to go, he ultimately decided on home and called his dad.

"Dad, can I come visit. Maybe, for a few days . . . maybe a week."

Even if Byron's voice hadn't been trembling and on the verge of tears, his father's answer would have been the same. "I can't wait to see you. You tell me when and I'll be at the airport. I could use a break also, perhaps fishing?"

And that is exactly how it went, and here they were doing their favorite father-son activity.

The thing that made fishing so popular for both Byron and his dad was that it didn't require talking. Byron loved that his dad was never pushing him to say what was going on in his life. In high school his friends said that trips with their fathers were excuses for an inquisition. How's school? Who's your best friend? What's your favorite class? Like any girls? But Byron's dad never pushed. Byron enjoyed that in his youth but now he wished his dad would make an exception.

Byron didn't want to admit it, but he needed to talk. After an hour in silence, he realized that if he needed conversation it would be incumbent on him to take the lead. "Dad, um . . . there are some things I wanted to talk to you about."

"Okay, Byron. I'm not going anywhere."

"Dad, did you ever have any tough times with mom?"

"Sure, everyone has tough times. No marriage is perfect."

"Well, things are definitely not perfect with Julie and me." Byron waited for the follow up questions, but they never came. Dad was not one to pry any further than he was offered. So, Byron finally said, "She wants a divorce."

"Oh, I'm sorry to hear that." He stayed calm but sadness showed in his face. He slowly reeled in his line, pulled it up to see that there was still some bait and then made a gentle cast out into the perfect stillness. "Do you want a divorce?"

"No, not really. In fact, I really had planned on telling her that I loved her when she asked for a divorce," Byron said.

"You have been married for a while now, haven't you told her that you love her before?"

"No, I haven't." Byron decided it was time to fill his father in on some of the complexities of his marriage.

An hour later, Byron's dad was more or less up to speed. He knew about how they had met, why they had married, their recent mechanical dating, and even about Charles.

"So, did you date her only because your father-in-law asked, or did you enjoy the time with her?"

"I loved dating her, like I said, I planned to tell her I loved her, and I do. I love her, I love spending time with her. But I feel like I can't stop her from having a chance to date someone else, if she really wants to. What can I do?" Byron asked.

"Son, there is something I think you should know. Something I think your mother would want you to know." Byron's heart was as still as the water in front of him. The tone was something he had never heard before. "When you were a senior in college, your mother had an affair."

"What?"

"She had gone to work full-time after you left for college and found herself regularly traveling with her boss for work."

"Was that why she quit that law firm?"

"Yes, after the affair she felt guilty, quit her job and came to me on bended knee, begging for forgiveness." He reeled in his line, picked his pole out of the water, set it down in the boat, and turned to Byron. "I didn't want to forgive her. I was bitter and unwilling to face the truth. The truth that I, for years, took her for granted, ignored her needs, and her dreams. I knew the affair was as much my fault as hers, but it was easier to blame, and embrace my bitterness. I knew everyone would be on my side, all I would have to say was, 'she cheated,' and everyone would understand. So, I began working with an attorney on the divorce. He had dropped papers off at my office for me to take home and sign. I walked in one night with those papers in my hand. Your mother had no idea.

"I had a chip on my shoulder bigger than me. And I hadn't been in the house five minutes before I was upset and arguing. She had been out all day at interviews and looking for a job so hadn't gotten to dinner. It's hard for me to admit, but I said, 'at least at the last job when you didn't have time to make dinner you helped pay for it, even if you were sleeping with your boss.'

"That's when the phone rang. Your mother let it ring a few times as she tried to cover the tears. She answered and I could tell it was you. I started to head to my study, since I assumed you wanted to talk to her. I was surprised when she stopped me and said you wanted to talk to me. It was the first time that I recall you calling and asking for me, when it wasn't my birthday.

"'Dad,' you said, 'I have decided what I want to be.' You were so excited that I couldn't even bring myself to say, 'Couldn't you figure this out before your senior year in college?' So, I simply asked you, 'What?' and you said, 'marriage counselor.'

"Of all the things you could have said at that moment you said, 'marriage counselor.'

"'Why son?' I asked. I don't know if you remember what you said, but I will never forget it. You said, 'Because of you, Dad. Because of you and Mom. I know your marriage isn't perfect but you work it out. Through good and bad, you work it out. I want to give people what you have. So many people give up so quickly on their marriage. I want to give them what you have.' Those words. 'I want to give them what you have.' You probably didn't repeat it ten times, but that's how many times I heard it. It kept going over and over in my head. My son was basing his career for the rest of his life on giving people what I had. And what did I have? An unfaithful wife, a broken marriage, anger, and resentment. I felt that I had nothing.

"Yet you thought I had something to share with the world, something worth saving. There was a huge divide between what I thought I had and what you thought I had. 'If only he knew, really understood,' I thought. I stayed up late into the night debating calling you, to let you know that if you planned to spend your life giving people what I had, that you were going to waste your career. I wanted to let you know that your mother and I were over, but I couldn't bring myself to do it. I was somewhere between praying and yelling at God when I muttered, 'Do I have anything worth saving?' and I heard a voice. I don't think it was an angel or anything but a voice said so clearly in my head, 'Yes. Your son is right. You do have something worth saving.'

"I wept more than I had in years and began to realize for the first time, so many things I had been blind to. I knelt down and asked God to help me see what you and He saw in my marriage. I cried, I prayed, and at some point during that restless night, I took the papers I had brought home and burned them. It wasn't easy, but from that moment I began to build the trust, forgiveness, and love that I had spent years tearing down.

"The night your mother lay dying in the hospital. I remember looking over at her so grateful for that night. So grateful for your career and what you were doing. You had saved me from wrecking my life, and had given me years of joy that I would not trade for every cent I ever had. I have always been proud of you son, and particularly because you are doing the most important things any human being can do, saving the most precious thing this world has to offer, family.

"Now, I know that you and Julie are not exactly your typical family. But honestly, in that regard, you are like everyone else."

Byron laughed as he wiped his nose and eyes, "What is that supposed to mean?"

"All I mean is, no one is typical. All our families are weird and unique. But what is important is they are ours. And what you taught me is that no matter how far gone you think they may be, no matter how much you think you don't have something worth saving, you have more than you realize. At least, I am so thankful that a young, want-to-be marriage counselor helped me decide to recognize and save what I had. And I think, no matter what happens, you will always regret it if you don't try to save what you have."

Byron allowed the moment, thoughts, and words to all set in. "Dad, do you mind if we call it a day and I get a ride to the airport. I think I better get home."

The engine was started before Byron could finish, "Aye-aye captain," his dad said as they headed for shore.

Chapter 23

The Breakup

Byron landed in Las Vegas with almost no plan of action, except that he was going to take some. A four-hour flight is a long time to be alone with your thoughts, and he spent the whole time debating what to say if he actually got ahold of Julie. Bare his heart out and hope for the best was his first idea. He went over and over again what he would say, but no matter how many different things he tried, he envisioned her saying, "That's nice. I still want Charles."

The next thought was to figure out what she saw in this Charles. Was it as simple as Charles being willing to take a little action? He was convinced he was ripe for improvement in this area. On the other hand, if it had more to do with the shape of Charles's nose or left bicep when compared to his, he doubted he could do much. But again, the more he analyzed this method, the more he thought that asking Julie "What does Charles got that I don't got?" might only lead to a very depressing conversation.

The next plan was to simply roll the dice on things not working out with Charles. Couldn't he give her the latitude to date and hope that it didn't work out? After all, once she dated Charles for a while, she may find she didn't like Charles any more than she liked him. And since she was already married to Byron, she could just save on lawyer fees and the cost of a new wedding and keep things as they were. But this too was found wanting. For some reason telling Julie they should stay married but date other people seemed icky. Logical as the idea seemed, he doubted that he could suggest it and doubted even more that Julie would go for it. Even suggesting it would only lead Julie to think less of him.

But even without a specific plan he wanted to do something and something today. It had cost him almost a thousand dollars to get a flight from St. Paul to Las Vegas and he was determined to get his money's worth. Step one, he figured, was locating Julie. As he walked off the plane, he sat down and dialed Julie. His goal was getting a face-to-face meeting but he knew his best chance in determining where she was, began with the phone. Julie's schedule was fairly predictable on a Saturday afternoon. It was usually that she was at home, with Becky, or with him. But these were pre-Charles days. The phone rang and rang. In some ways this was good. Byron really didn't know what he would say except, "We need to talk." Something he could just as easily deliver to an answering machine, which he did. But he had not paid almost a grand to get back home simply to leave a message, something he could have done from a distance.

So, onto step two. He called her again. Same outcome. Step three, one more time, but this time there wasn't even a ring as it went straight to voicemail. Before he proved the definition of insanity, he decided to try something different and sent her a text, saying the same thing. While staring at his phone, it rang, but it wasn't Julie's number.

"Hello."

"Byron?"

"Yes, this is he. Who is this?"

"Byron, son, this is your father-in-law, Pelham."

"Hi. I have to admit that I'm surprised to hear from you."

"Well, truth is, I should have called you a few days ago, but it took me a while to find your number, and Julie wasn't in the mood to give it to me."

"How did you get my number?" Byron asked.

"You know your secretary is really nice. She gave it to me yesterday. I tried to call you then but it went straight to voicemail."

Byron had told her about giving people his personal cell phone, but he had said patients so he guessed this case was a fair loophole. "I was on a plane to Minnesota."

"Well I'm glad I got a hold of you. The reason I called Byron is, remember how I said to you that you shouldn't tell her I was involved in you two going out?" Pelham asked.

"Well she found out and it's really bad."

"She told me," Byron said

"Were you able to smooth it out?"

"She wants a divorce."

"I guess that is a no. She can be really stubborn sometimes. Gets that from her mother. So, how do you feel about this divorce?"

"Truth is sir, I love that stubborn woman and don't want a divorce," Byron said.

"I knew I liked you. So, what's the game plan? For one, you should probably get back from Minnesota."

"I am back."

"That was quick. I thought you flew there yesterday."

"I flew yesterday to help get over Julie, woke up at four a.m. to go fishing, realized I needed to try to get back and save my marriage, so flew right back," Byron explained.

"Sounds like a productive trip. So, what is your game plan?"

"I thought I'd try to start by finding Julie, she's not answering her phone."

"She wouldn't pick up for me right now anyways, so don't ask me to call. But are you sure finding Julie is the best choice right now?" Pelham asked.

"What do you mean?"

"Go ahead, what would you tell her if you walked up to her right now?"

"I . . . would . . . um . . . say . . . Julie, why can't we . . . go ahead . . . and . . . this time . . ."

"My point exactly. You need to wow her, have an impactful romantic moment, not dribble over your tongue."

"I figured it would come to me, what to say," Byron tried justifying his lack of eloquence.

"All men think that. And centuries of experience has taught us that it doesn't work. You need a romantic, planned moment, Byron, and some local help. I think I know what to do."

Julie couldn't have been more excited for today. Charles had decided to take her back to the cabin site and have a picnic. She hadn't had a picnic since she was a teenager. The fact that Charles was being so creative for their date really added to the excitement. Byron never thought of anything but watching something and going to dinner. Julie had asked what they were going to have but Charles said it would be a surprise. Not only that, she couldn't help but be excited about a date with the prospect of more than just talking.

Pre-kiss with Charles she had to go back three years to her wedding night to find any time she had really had any affection, and that was only a kiss on the cheek. And now she had cleared away that pesky problem of guilt. True, she was still technically married, but having asked Byron for a divorce, she felt like she could reasonably say she was on the market. She was as free as a bird. Tonight she couldn't guarantee anything, but at least for the first time in a long time, there was a chance. She was reflecting on how she had taken this chance so much for granted back when she was single as she tried on her second outfit, that's when the phone rang.

"Hi, Beck."

"So, did you work out the details with Smooth Charlie?"

"Are you ever going to drop that name?"

"No, I like it," Becky said.

"Well, the answer is yes, Charles is going to pick me up at about four."

"What's the plan?"

"Picnic under the sunset at his cabin site."

"Romantic. It's going to be fairly chilly up there, you better bring a jacket. Actually, maybe you shouldn't."

"Right," Julie said.

"So, Julie, not to change the subject, but I was wondering after your talk with Byron."

"Yes?"

"Does he want another wife?" Becky asked.

"What?"

"It's just that having a husband that is willing to simply send you money is a pretty good deal. I mean, I thought it was crazy to answer him in the first place, but now that we know he is actually a decent guy, seems like a pretty good arrangement."

"Do you want me to put in a good word for you?" Julie joked.

"Hey now, I am very happily, alright mostly, maybe I should say sometimes, happily married to Mark. But that is not the point. It's not for me. But you know Sandra, she could use a good man and a little extra money."

"Are you serious? You want to set Byron up with Sandra Hilterford. They would never get along."

"I didn't realize getting along was a prerequisite. And what about Nellie?" Becky suggested.

"Nellie? Your neighbor with the twelve cats?"

"It might work out."

"What has gotten into you? Why would you want to set up Byron?" Julie really didn't feel comfortable about this. Byron was a good guy but he was meant to be single. She thought it was best that way.

"You know me, I love matchmaking," Becky said.

"Isn't it a little weird to be setting up my ex?"

"Don't take any offense to this but the more I thought about Byron's idea, the more I liked it. I mean, sure it didn't work out for you two, but I think there are lots of people that it would be great for."

"We are not even really divorced yet."

"That isn't stopping Smooth Charlie," Becky said.

"Oh, okay. That's a low blow. Things are a little different for Charles and me."

"And how is that?"

"Because, I asked for the divorce. I don't even know if he wants to get married again. In fact, I don't think he does," Julie said.

"You know it sounds like you might be a little jealous."

"That is crazy. I am anything but jealous of some imaginary future Byron bride. I wish him the best. But I am not going to call him up and ask him if my friend can set him up."

"Of course not, that would be crazy." Julie was glad to see Becky was a little reasonable. "Give me his number. I'll call him."

"No." She realized the quick rejection of the idea was too fast, too harsh. "I'll think about it. But I need to go. I want to try on a few more options to get the perfect outfit. And your conversation is not helping me get in the right mood."

"Okay. You have fun with Smooth Charlie. I want the details when you get home tonight," Becky said.

"I'll think about that too. See ya."

"Bye."

She hung up and tried to focus on her outfit, but she kept thinking about Byron. Was she jealous? She didn't think so, but she really didn't like the thought of him with anyone else. "No more thoughts about Byron!" she stated out loud to herself, hoping that would help her mind actually listen. "Tonight is about Charles and me." She looked at the next outfit when the phone rang. It was Byron. She didn't need this and sent the call to voicemail. Soon a notification on her phone told her that he had left a voicemail and the phone began to ring again. She wanted to be left alone to focus on Charles and so, after sending the phone to voicemail again, she shut the phone off. With the distractions gone, she got ready to focus on today. Three outfits later, she was ready to go.

Shortly after four o'clock, that beautiful Porsche pulled up and Charles honked. She figured he would come to the door, but that was fine. "You ready for this?" Charles asked as she hopped in. She instantly smelled the aroma of fried food.

"What did you get for the picnic?" Julie asked.

"Hot wings," Charles said with excitement.

"That's great," Julie said as honestly as one who hated hot wings could muster. But then again, she hadn't said she had come for the food. Hopefully the rest of the night would be better.

"Is that the door?" Becky asked her husband. They hadn't invited anyone and it was too late for a package. She went to the door. "Byron. What are you doing here?"

"Sorry to bother you, but I need to talk to you and I didn't know your phone number, but I remembered where you lived from the book club. I hope this isn't a bad time."

"No, come on in. Did Julie change her mind about letting me talk to you?"

"Julie wanted me to talk to you?" Byron asked.

"No, I told Julie that I wanted to talk to you and for her to give me your phone number. But I guess sending you over is just as good."

"Julie didn't send me. Why did you want to talk to me?"

"Well . . . " Setting him up with her friends had seemed like a good idea but she wasn't sure how to bring it up. "I was thinking with you and Julie ending, maybe you would be interested to be set up with a few of my friends."

"Really?" Byron collected his thoughts, "Actually, I was hoping you would help me. Can you tell me where Julie is?"

"Why do you care?" Becky asked.

"I would like to speak to her."

"Before I agree to help you, I need to ask you something."

"You want me to go on a date with one of your friends first?" Byron asked.

"No, that's not it." She paused. "Actually, yes it is."

"Really?" Byron asked.

"For me to help, you have to agree to go on one date with a friend."

"I'm not doing that," stated Byron

"Well, goodbye then."

"I really need your help."

"Then, one date," Becky countered.

"I can't believe I am agreeing to this."

"Excellent, I almost wish I could make it two because then there would be room for Nellie, the cat lady. She'd leave you with an interesting story. I heard she has a couple cats as sympathy animals, I'd love to hear how dinner goes with those things crawling around. But she isn't who I had in mind. "But besides that," she continued, "I have another question. Are you gay?"

"No, why would you think I was gay?" Byron asked.

"All this time dating Julie and she said you two never . . . you know."

"Wow, you two are close. No, I'm not gay, just gutless, I guess."

"But with you here on my front door, I'm guessing you grew some guts, and are now trying to recapture Julie," Becky said and Byron nodded.

"Now will you answer a question of mine? You two being so close, do you know how serious she is with this Charles guy?"

"You mean Smooth Charlie. I shouldn't tell you this, after all you two are competing for Julie, so I probably shouldn't give any insider information. I don't want it to be an unfair fight. But two things you should know: she is with him now, and I don't trust him."

"Why not?" Byron asked.

"She went to dinner with him once, supposedly to talk 'work' or something and they ended up kissing. Anyone that smooth has had a bit too much practice, you know what I mean."

"I guess. But this guy is pretty good at this 'being smooth' thing, huh?"

"Not only that, he is really good looking. You should hear Julie talk about him, perfect hair, face, tall, muscular, and he drives this really nice Porsche."

"All right," Byron's stomach was beginning to feel like it did at the wedding. "I think we better change the topic," he said.

"You do have one thing on him."

"And that is?" Byron lit up.

"Your last name is normal. He's named after a department store."

"Wait, his name is Charles Nordstrom?"

"Yup, that's it. You know him?" Becky asked.

"No, but I know his wife."

Julie was surprised to find that she didn't hate the chicken wings, luckily not all of them were hot and he had brought celery and carrots with bleu cheese dressing too. She also wondered if the atmosphere was adding to the taste. The mountain was, as expected, the perfect relief from the city heat. The air was beginning to chill as the sun began to fall down behind the peak. Charles's company, as usual, was as thrilling as ever and he was telling about an archaeological dig he had been on in Africa.

"At first, I was nervous about the lions wandering the site, but I got used to them. One day I turned a corner and ran smack into one of the larger males. You should have seen him run, he must have been related to the lion from Alice in Wonderland, just a big scaredy cat."

As he told the story he moved in closer to where Julie was sitting. She was hanging onto his every word and didn't even mind that he didn't know one children's story from another. "Are you getting chilly?" Charles asked as he scooted next to her.

"It is getting a little cold," she said, even though it wasn't yet. As planned, he took his jacket and wrapped it and his large arms around her. She leaned into his chest and they nuzzled against each other. With each breath he took in she could feel his muscular chest push against her face. This was nice, this is what she wanted. She decided to move things along even more. "Charles, I asked Byron for a divorce."

He pulled slightly away from her as he looked down at her. "Why would you do that?"

"What do you mean, why would I do that?" Julie asked.

"Yeah, why?"

"Because of you."

"I'm not sure I follow," Charles said.

"You kissed me earlier this week and then brought me on a picnic to watch the sunset," she said as she sat up.

"Yeah, so why divorce your husband?"

"I can't believe this. You did all that and expected me to just stay married?"

"Hey, when you told me about your marriage it seemed like it was more like a convenience thing, not about love."

"But you were fine with me just keeping it going?" When Julie thought that her heart might be racing tonight, this was not what she had in mind.

"Sure, it was kind of perfect. You were married for convenience but that wouldn't stop you and me from having a thing. And it wouldn't tie me down. I mean, technically, I'm married too."

"You're married?!" Julie yelled as she stood up.

"Whoa, I don't think you have any moral high ground here. You are married too, remember."

"Does she know you are out schmoozing with, I'd say some hussy if I wasn't talking about myself?"

"We are more on and off. I'm sure she would understand. And don't look at me like that, my marriage is less of a sham than yours is."

"My marriage to Byron is not a sham. I may have been a little confused, something you didn't help with, but I will have you know that my marriage may have been weird, or unconventional but we were friends. And that is a lot more than many people get in marriage." As soon as she said the words, she knew they were true. She wasn't sure if she was madder at Charles or herself. She instantly was beginning to realize that while what she had with Byron wasn't perfect, it wasn't worth throwing away.

And she was willing to throw it aside for what? A smooth, married player who went around preying on married women. Why had she fallen so fast? She had barely known him. Her anger was turning into tears and she wondered what she could possibly do at this point. She was determined not to get back in the car with this Smooth Charlie, but saw little option. It was over an hour drive from her house, and if she walked off, it would soon be dark and cold. She was desperate and in her desperation she began to pray in her mind, "Please don't make me have to spend any more time with this guy."

She was halfway through this thought when a red SUV pulled up far faster than it should. It stopped almost in time to avoid any damage to Charles's Porsche, but almost, unfortunately does not save the bumpers of small sports cars when they meet their much larger friends.

"My car!" Charles yelled out.

Becky jumped out. "Julie you are coming with me," she demanded, in as commanding a voice as she could muster.

"Gladly," Julie said as she ran towards the passenger seat.

"Well, that was a lot easier than I thought it would be," Becky said. "Charlie, it was good to meet you," she smiled as she hopped back into her car.

"What are you going to do about my car?" he whined. But it was too late, Becky was pulling away.

Chapter 24

Final Blind Date

"How did you know I needed you to pick me up?" Julie said, as they drove away from Charles cabin site.

"I guess I didn't," Becky said in reply. "But I did know that Charles was bad news."

"What do you mean you knew he was bad news? If you did, you could have said something before I went up on a secluded mountain picnic with him."

"I didn't know he was bad news until Byron told me about his wife. Did you know Smooth Charlie was married?" Becky asked.

"I do now. How did you end up talking to Byron, and how does he know Charles is married?"

"Byron made me promise that I not say anything, since he wasn't supposed to tell me anything about Charles's wife. And I guess he didn't tell me anything about her except that she existed, which was all I really needed to know."

"Did you find Byron's number and try to set him up already?"

"No," Becky said defensively. "I mean I would have but you wouldn't give me his number, remember."

"Well, if you didn't reach out to him, how did you two get together?" Julie asked.

"He stopped by."

"What?"

"It's not important, but I did get to talk to him about my plan to set him up." Becky was a wizard at changing topics that she knew would get Julie riled up.

"You didn't?"

"He was more open to the idea than you might think."

This was not the news Julie wanted. "I can't imagine that he was willing to be set up."

"He actually asked me to set him up with a particular person. Sounds like with you wanting a divorce, he's ready to move on."

"That seems a little fast. Who did he want you to set him up with?"

"He made me promise not to tell. But what do you care?"

"Well, with how things worked out with Charles," Julie paused, she knew what she needed to say, but hated the taste of crow. "I thought maybe divorce was a little hasty."

"Do you really want Byron back?"

"Yes, so please don't set him up."

It was Becky's turn to be hesitant. "I kind of, already did."

"What, when is he going on this date of his?"

"Tomorrow."

"I can't believe you set my husband up on a date with someone."

"Hey, you are the one who tried to divorce him."

"He could've waited for the divorce to be final before he started shopping for a new wife."

"You didn't," Becky shot back.

"Okay, fine, is this date set up thing him trying to get a new convenience wife, or is this him actually wanting a real date?"

"I think after trying the marriage of convenience thing, he's looking for the real deal," Becky admitted.

"Why would you say that? Even if it's true, just lie to me. What am I going to do now?"

"If you want him back, you should fight for him," Becky suggested.

"How do you expect me to do that? Show up at his date, sock some unknown friend of yours in the nose and then profess my undying love for the man I told I wanted a divorce a few days before?"

"Well, it's not a perfect plan, but it's not bad either."

"Does this friend of yours have a soft face?"

"She is pretty."

"I don't care about looks. I want to know if her face is soft. I don't want to break my hand on her nose. So, really, who is she?"

"I have been sworn to secrecy."

"Like that ever stopped you," Julie said.

"Now I'm offended and for sure won't tell. But I do know where they are meeting."

"You really expect me to break up the date you set him up on?"

"Why not? Worth a try."

"Did I ever tell you that you are the worst best friend ever?"

"I do my best."

"Where are they going?" Julie asked.

"It's a little cafe in the Bellagio."

Julie walked briskly through the casino, she was torn between whether her punch would be better placed on this mystery girl or on Byron. When Becky had told her that he had chosen the place they had first met for his date with this girl, she was furious. She realized Byron probably didn't think twice about it. Most likely he simply liked their pesto spread, but she couldn't get it out of her mind that while still married to her he was going to take some other girl, not only on a date, but to the place where they first met.

She realized she couldn't be too upset, after all, she had asked for the divorce, but the more she walked, the more she thought about it, and the more she thought about it the more upset she became. She had worked up quite a head of steam by the time she rolled around to see Byron sitting at a table all alone. She couldn't believe it—he had a rose pinned on his shirt. This only added to her anger. She went straight up to him and demanded, "Where is she?"

"Julie!" Byron said with surprise, "I didn't expect you."

"I am sure you didn't. So, where is she? Did she run off to the bathroom, or is she running late?" Julie demanded.

"Late, I guess. Did Becky tell you where I would be?"

"Are you embarrassed about dating, while still married to me?" The few heads in the store were now all facing their way.

"I thought you wanted a divorce?"

"If every couple you counseled gave up at the first mention of divorce, how many would still be married?"

"Good point. And given that, I have something I want to say to you."

She paused to listen and after an extended silence she said, "Well . . .?"

"Julie," he took a deep breath and got down on one knee. "I love you. I don't want us to get divorced. If you are willing to get rid of Charles, I promise to cherish you the way I should. I should have fought for you a long time ago. It wasn't until I almost lost you that I realized what I have. I love our time together and I want you to be my wife, I mean, for real this time."

The crowd couldn't have been more pleased with the performance. That is, except for the last line which left them a little confused. Julie on the other hand loved every word.

"You mean it?" She couldn't stop the water from forming around the edges of her eyes.

"Very much so."

"Well then?" she said looking into his eyes.

"Well then what?" Byron asked.

She looked at him and he realized what it was he was supposed to do. He stood, pulled her into his arms, and they, for the first time, kissed, really kissed . . . and kissed and kissed again.

At some point during a breath, she slapped him on the chest and asked, "What about you wanting to get set up with one of Becky's friends?"

"What, she told me I had to go on a date with one of her friends or she wouldn't help me get you back. The only friend of Becky's I wanted was you."

They kissed again as Julie heard a text come through.

Looking down at her phone, they both noticed it was from Becky.

"I hope you like the girl I set Byron up with. Your dad and I thought you two would get along."

They smiled as they fell back into each other's arms.

"You wouldn't understand. You haven't been there. I don't care how many degrees you have, it's not the same until you have dealt with it yourself. I'm sorry. We're leaving."

The couple stood and walked out of Byron's office. They continued their bit of a storm, through the waiting room as Julie walked in. "What was that all about?"

"Oh, they are having trouble with their kid, and don't want advice from me, someone with *no experience*. I thought about solving this the same way I have in the past, but an ad in the paper looking for a child may get me into trouble."

"Didn't you cover in school how to help people with parenting issues?"

"Sure, but supposedly no class is good enough."

"Well funny, that's why I'm stopping by. I wanted to let you know that you and I just enrolled in a class that might do the trick."

She held up the only stick that you are allowed to pee on and then keep as a souvenir. They kissed and then ran into the lobby to tell Mrs. Goodman the good news.

About the Author

The only thing Nathaniel Gee loves more than writing is supporting his wife and eight children, which is why he works as a Dam Safety Engineer. His determination to become a writer came from an inspirational school counselor who said that he would be a much better engineer than a writer. He was a well-loved writer of his local newspaper and continues writing on his blog at www.thegeebrothers.com, professional journals in Dam Safety, and in his favorite genres—romantic comedy and detective fiction. He also has a YouTube channel, Geelightful, where his children are far more popular than he is. You can reach out to Nathaniel or check out what else he is up to at nathanielkgee.com.

Scan to visit

nathanielkgee.com